Mary Watson

In the Shadow of Sherlock Holmes

The Adventures of Mary Morstan Watson

by

Stefano Guerra

Enrico Solito

Mauro Castellini

Gian Luca Guerra

Supervision of the translation by Alfredo Scott Hamill

Hardcover ISBN 978-1-80424-369-5
Paperback ISBN 978-1-80424-370-1

Published by MX Publishing
335 Princess Park Manor, Royal Drive,
London, N11 3GX
www.mxpublishing.co.uk

Cover design by Brian Belanger

Contents

THE DISCOVERY OF A VOCATION

1.   Alone in the World

In 1878, at the boarding school in Edinburgh where I had lived since I was a child, I received a letter from my father, Captain Morstan, who was stationed in the Andaman Islands, India. After the death of my mother, I had been sent home to Great Britain because lacking maternal guidance, it was considered the only place where I would be safely cared for and receive a proper education. However, my father never failed to be present in my life, even if only through letters.

In that letter, as affectionate as always, he informed me of his retirement from the service and arranged to meet me in London at the Langham Hotel on the day he would arrive. A few weeks later, a telegram informed me of his arrival, and I rushed to London with a tumultuous heart. However, what happened shocked me and remained a great mystery for a long time: my father had arrived but, after going out the night before, he never returned. I waited for him all day without any news. Together with the hotel manager, we searched for clues in his luggage, full of curiosities and memories from the Andaman Islands, but found nothing. I reported his disappearance to the police that same evening and placed an advertisement in the newspapers. In the following days, I tried every possible avenue, including speaking with Major Sholto, a friend and former comrade of my father, but it was all in vain. My father had disappeared like a stone sinking in a river, and I was forced to return to the school in Edinburgh, whose tuition had already been paid until I reached adulthood.

The disappointment was excruciating, especially for a girl who suddenly found herself alone in the world, forced to forge her own future without anyone preparing it for her. Those were mentally challenging years, but I refused to be defeated. I discovered that my resilience was greater than I had ever believed.

A few years later, as my time in Edinburgh came to an end, I embarked on a new path, perhaps the only dignified one available to an orphan with limited means: with the help of the school, I found employment as a governess in the house of Mrs. Violet Cecil Forrester in London. Mrs. Forrester, more than an employer, proved to be almost like a friend, showing immediate concern for me and making me feel cared for like never before. This warmed my heart and filled me with joy, motivating me even more to do everything in my power to live up to the task entrusted to me. I lived in peace and serenity for several months until a fateful day in May 1882.

2. From Mary's Diary

London, May 4, 1882
I was surprised to read an anonymous advertisement in The Times seeking my address, informing me that it would be advantageous for me to come forward. Having nothing to hide, I discussed it with Mrs. Forrester and decided to respond. This afternoon, I received a small box in the mail, which, to my great surprise, contained a large pearl with a marvelous glow, without a message, a word, or a clue that could lead me to the name of the donor.

London, May 4, 1883

One year later, another pearl arrived in a similar box, once again without a single line of comment. This situation is becoming increasingly difficult to bear. Not only has my father's disappearance remained an open wound in my heart, but the presence of a mysterious person who feels compelled to send me such a precious object without an explanation could push someone more fragile and prone to imagination to the brink of madness. I discussed at length with my friend and landlady about the possible hypotheses behind these deliveries.

London, July 7, 1888

Once again, this year, in May, the mysterious pearl arrived, as has happened for the past six years. However, this time there is something new: the pearl was followed, a couple of months later, by an equally mysterious letter promising to reveal all the details of this story if I went to a certain place accompanied by two friends, who must not belong to the police force. Since my father's disappearance, I have found no peace. Could it be that the time has finally come to learn the truth about his fate? What if he is somehow involved?

I discussed it with Violet again, and she insists that I should do everything humanly possible to unravel this mystery. She argues that if I were someone else, capable of accepting the considerable fortune that is being revealed to me bit by bit without asking further questions, she would advise me to let it go and accept what fate brings. But she knows me too well now to know that this worry is capable of poisoning my existence. She recommended that I turn to an acquaintance of hers, a sort of private consulting detective who has been very helpful to her in the past. His name is Sherlock Holmes. I can't take this tension any longer, so I've decided to go see him today.

London, July 8, 1888

Yesterday afternoon, I was received by Mr. Sherlock Holmes, a decidedly interesting person with a clearly superior intelligence. He was courteous, very professional, clearly interested in what I had to say, but his gaze wandered into space as I spoke, as if searching somewhere for the possibility of organizing the things I was telling him. Then, suddenly, his gray eyes fixed on me, never losing sight of me for a moment, and I couldn't help but feel embarrassed. It wasn't the gaze of a man observing a woman; there was no interest in me as a person. I felt observed like a scientist would observe, I would say, an entomologist.

With him was the person introduced to me as his colleague, Dr. John Watson, who had a completely different attitude. He was a very kind person, almost gallant. Reserved, when he realized I was talking about a matter that deeply affected me, he was about to leave, and it was me who begged him to stay. Robust, while the other appears as fragile as a reed, solid, slightly limping, his mustache reminds me a bit of my father. Perhaps the fact that he had been a military man gave me the sense that I could trust him. The other one impressed me with his perspicacity and i could feel that my logical side resonated with him immediately, but the doctor seemed like the kind of man you could rely on without fear of him causing harm. He didn't take his eyes off me, certainly with a gaze very different from Sherlock Holmes'. I would describe it as captivated, devoted, enraptured. Embarrassing in its own way as well. However, he made it clear to me not only that he had perceived my emotional difficulties but also that he would be ready to take care of my fragility.

Sherlock Holmes, too, was ready to take on my case, but as an intellectual matter, as a mental challenge between himself and the enigma that I brought to his attention.

John Watson understood me, seeing beyond my problem.

Another interesting person in this peculiar family is the landlady, Mrs. Hudson. A widow, I believe. She, too, has been very welcoming and courteous, and I appreciate her ability to take care of others. The attention she paid to making me feel comfortable and ensuring that everything ran smoothly, while also being able to stand up to Sherlock Holmes's idiosyncrasies and eccentricities, has won me over. I would like to be a person who knows how to take care of others like this lady does. A fine example of womanhood.

3.   The Sign of the Four

I have transcribed above the pages of my diary that concern the beginning of that strange and, for me, shocking affair, which later became known as "The Sign of Four," as recounted by Dr. John Watson. That day, as I left the apartment on Baker Street, struck by the personalities of the two gentlemen I had just met, I felt supported and reassured for the first time in facing a difficult ordeal. I returned home feeling slightly relieved.

When I arrived, I found Mrs. Forrester in a state of agitation, like a hive of busy bees. She took my hands and forced me to sit down and tell her everything. Her curiosity was not mere nosiness but genuine interest, which warmed my heart. I gladly recounted everything: my impressions of the detective and his kind and competent friend, Dr. Watson; the expertise with which Mr. Holmes examined the envelopes and messages and the deductions he made from them; the approving look he gave me for being precise in my narrative and for bringing not only the letter but all the packages I had received over the years.

"Oh, Mary, you are extraordinary. I could never be as attentive and precise as you, let alone. So, you will return to them and go together. I'll stay awake for you, my dear, and I must confess I am quite agitated."

"Thank you, Violet, but now calm down. It's almost four o'clock, and it's time for me to give your children their lessons. I still have to earn my salary, I think!"

Being with the children helped me control the increasing tension I felt as the time for the mysterious meeting approach. When I reappeared at Baker Street, wrapped in a dark cloak, I had the awareness that, despite my pounding heart, I was completely in control of myself. Mr. Holmes carefully examined a strange sheet that I had found among my father's papers: a kind of map signed with a cross and four names that I was unfamiliar with, three of which were certainly Asian. He told me the paper was Indian, but otherwise, the mystery was absolute.

The fog grew thicker in the streets as our carriage headed to the appointed location. Sherlock Holmes fell into a gloomy silence, and his friend, on the other hand, engaged in a friendly and polite conversation, undoubtedly attempting to distract me. He was a handsome man, with a solid appearance and a compassionate and loyal gaze, a man ready to put himself at the disposal of an unknown girl to protect and help her out of a sense of chivalry, sensing the curious mix of nervousness and melancholy that tormented me. That evening, a feeling of gratitude and friendship began to grow in me, which would only increase over time.

What followed was told much better by Dr. Watson himself in his account of our adventure. I remember the barely controlled pounding of my heart as I waited in the foggy crowd outside the theater. I was surprised to be approached by a sort of driver and invited to join with my companions in a carriage that then took off on a mad race through streets I couldn't recognize. And then, the figure of Dr. Watson, who continued to speak incessantly during the long journey to the outskirts. I barely managed to control my tension as we entered a strange house, an environment both oppressive and laden with strange aromas, abounding in carpets, tiger skins, and Oriental furniture. It felt as if I were living in a dream, unsure whether it would turn into a nightmare or a moment of liberation. The question pulsating in my mind was: What happened to my father? Could he still be alive? And if so, why had he remained silent all these years? Or should I resign myself to the worst?

The blow struck by the fat, bald though youngish man who greeted us, who bluntly declared that my father was dead, was swift and brutal, but at least it shattered any illusions: Deep down, I had known the truth and yet I confess I faltered, collapsing with a pale face into a chair. That was Thaddeus, one of Major Sholto's two sons. He tended to ramble, and I couldn't follow the thread of his speech. I had to apologize and insistently ask him to get to the point before he decided to do so.

However incredible his story was, it shook me and captured my attention. His father and mine had come into possession of a fabulous treasure brought from India to England by Sholto; my father, while discussing with his comrade on the very night he had arrived in London, had a heart attack and fell, hitting his head against a corner, and consequently died. If the police had been called, the ensuing investigation would likely have incriminated the Major, with the incident's dynamics appearing highly improbable. But, above all, it would have revealed the story of the treasure. Thus, to avoid trouble, the body had been made to disappear, and when, years later, Sholto had decided to reveal the matter to his sons, he, in turn, died immediately afterward, unable to disclose where the treasure was hidden. But finally, it had been found, and the time had come to return my share to me. It was the two Sholtos, Thaddeus and Bartholomew who had sent me the pearls over the years, part of what their father had left behind, but now it was a matter of hurrying to the brother's house, the family home in Norwood, to take possession of everything that was rightfully mine.

That very long night had just begun, and I found myself in the carriage again, dazed, saddened, and amazed to go from being a governess to a wealthy heiress, yet with a frozen heart: for the first time, what I feared had become a reality. I was alone in the world, completely alone. That was the thought tormenting my mind while Sholto, a real hypochondriac, tormented poor Dr. Watson throughout the journey, listing his ailments, while Holmes gazed into the night with a furrowed brow.

We arrived after eleven, and after gaining entrance at the gatehouse, we discovered the unimaginable. The grand house was dark, without a single light, except for a small window, the housekeeper's which appeared illuminated. From that direction came the sobs of a terrified woman who let Thaddeus Sholto in while we waited outside in the park, which was wrecked by holes dug everywhere evidently in the search for the treasure. Instinctively, I grasped the doctor's arm beside me. I later apologized, but my weeping in the dark of the night was the final outpouring of the frightening emotions of that night and being able to rely on him, to accept his hand holding mine, to seek comfort and protection from him, was so natural for me that I still marvel at it today.

In an instant, we were inside the house, in the room of the terrified housekeeper who was trembling like a leaf. It was instinctive for me to approach her and reassure her, calming her, while the men went upstairs to see what had happened to Bartholomew Sholto.

I spent a long time comforting that poor woman, who cried helplessly, but we could only speculate about what had happened. The arrival of the police, the commotion that engulfed the house, Thaddeus Sholto's coming and going gradually made it clear that Bartholomew Sholto had been murdered and the treasure stolen. I managed to remain calm and clear-minded until the end of that incredible night when Dr. Watson put me in a carriage to return to the Forresters' house in Lower Camberwell.

4.   From Mary's Diary

London, July 9, 1888

Last night, after such an overwhelming day, I burst into tears in the carriage in which Dr. Watson was bringing me back to Violet's. The tension of the day, Bartholomew's death, the theft of the treasure, the realization that I had been in personal danger and had put my new friends in danger as well, caused me to collapse after I had expended all my remaining energy to calm Mrs. Bernstone, the Sholto housekeeper. And while I cried desperately, inexplicably, Dr. Watson didn't say a word of comfort to me: He appeared cold and indifferent, staring out of the window, as if eager to arrive and leave me in Violet's care. What a disappointment, to have been so wrong about him! Fortunately, Violet welcomed me with her usual kindness: Even though it was two in the morning, she had stayed up waiting for me and tenderly accompanied me to bed. This morning, no one was around. I hope to have some more news in the afternoon.

London, July 10, 1888
Since this whole story began, my imagination has swung between the brightest prospects and the darkest outcomes. The fear that it would bring me immense suffering proved to be true, as I learned about the fate of my poor father, but no matter how much I let my imagination soar, I couldn't even dream of a happiness as intense as the one I've been feeling since last night. Yesterday, Violet allowed me to sleep in, so when Dr. Watson came in the afternoon to tell us about the latest developments of the investigation, I had regained my energy and even some cheerfulness. He also seemed more relaxed as he recounted in detail Sherlock Holmes's discoveries about the murderers' identities and declared his readiness to confront them alongside his friend. Violet was very impressed by the events, comparing them to the plot of a novel, and by the extent of the riches I could possess. I, however, was primarily anxious for poor Thaddeus to be quickly exonerated, unfairly accused of his brother's murder. I likened Mr. Holmes and Dr. Watson to two knights errant, engaged in a battle against evil to save the damsel in distress, and it seemed that the doctor didn't dislike the comparison at all.

When he left to join Holmes, I felt the weight of responsibility for the danger I had exposed both of them to, and I felt deeply grateful for their generosity. John Watson returned in the night to bring me the news of Jonathan Small's arrest, his accomplice's death, and the recovery of the treasure, locked in a chest that he brought with him, with the police's permission, so that I would be the first to see it. Once again, knowing in detail the risks he had taken for me unsettled and moved me, just as his modesty touched me. But the moment that will remain unforgettable for me, for the rest of my life, was when John forced open the lock of the chest and opened it, only to find it empty.

He thanked the Lord; he couldn't, didn't contain his joy in discovering that I was no longer fabulously wealthy and therefore no longer out of reach for him: "I love you, Mary," he said, "as truly as ever a man loved a woman!"
And we lost ourselves in each other's arms.

London, August 24, 1888
I feel as if I'm intoxicated with happiness. Violet, who claims she has never seen me like this before, urges me to hurry with the preparations for the wedding because "it's a crime to be so happy and still wait," and John would agree. But my pragmatism, instilled in me by the boarding school, reminds me that we need to find a house large enough for us and the children to come, with sufficient space for my husband's clinic (husband: a word that excites me). Yes, because the enthusiasm for the new life that awaits us has shaken John so profoundly that it has convinced him to return to his profession, and I am certain he will be an excellent doctor. So here I am, in the midst of summer, searching for houses while continuing to live with the Forresters, educating those adorable children. And already I can't help but think about when I will have my own to take care of! Will I be capable? I had no difficulties with other people's children, but I realize it's not so simple for Violet... may God help me.

London, September 16, 1888
These splendid summer days are ideal for taking the children to the park. I thought of studying botany "en plein air," right among the plants and shrubs. Books are too dry for them.

They seem happy with the novelty, and for a few days now, I've been wandering near the ponds, among children spinning hoops vigorously on the path and others launching ships from the shores, with nannies bringing the little ones to sunbathe and elderly ladies walking with careful dignity while hiding under their parasols.

Usually, these hours spent outdoors make me cheerful and carefree, and I have to make an effort not to let go completely and start running and laughing with the Forrester children like a silly girl ("you should do it, instead," Violet would tell me, always insisting on my excessive maturity). But today, I witnessed an unpleasant scene that saddened me throughout the day, and I want to record it here, in my diary, so as not to forget the details.

I have known Louise for a long time, a saleswoman at the glove and hat shop where Violet is a loyal customer, and where I also go when I need something. She is a girl of modest beauty, reserved, who gives me the impression that she fears being too forward, even by laughing, or appearing happy. While I was in the large open space of the park near the central lake, I saw her talking to a man accompanying her as they wandered about. He was a tanned young man with an open gaze and a determined manner.

I was about to approach and greet them when I noticed that something strange was happening. Louise continued to speak in a calm tone, but the man started raising his voice, taking a step back and staring at her sternly with an angry expression. From my position, I couldn't hear the words, but what I saw was enough to consider it a real argument, which ended when he rudely turned away, leaving the girl alone and in tears despite her attempts to hold him back. It was none of my business, of course, and I refrained from interfering in such a delicate situation, but I couldn't help but try to help that poor girl in some way. So I waited until the shops reopened and went to see her, using the excuse of buying a pair of gloves. I know well that in moments of distress, a smile, a kind word, warm the heart more than many speeches. So I approached the girl and asked her for what I needed, making sure to do it as gently as possible and with the intention of thanking her warmly for her kindness and competence. She must have appreciated it because those who are sad feel pleased when they are treated kindly. But as she turned to reach for the new pair of gloves, I had asked to see, her sleeve slightly pulled back, and I distinctly saw purple bruises on her wrist: the girl had been violently shaken. I left with a heavy heart, unable to do anything for her. I don't know the origin of the altercation, but her male friend is certainly a scoundrel.

London, September 18, 1888
I have discussed the incident regarding Louise, the young saleswoman at the glove shop, with Violet at length. I haven't even mentioned it to John: He is too much of a gentleman to even consider doing such a thing, but I know he would tell me that the law allows for it and more. Violet explained to me, to my horror, that a husband can even beat his wife without fearing any consequences. It's true that in this case, he's a fiancé, but it doesn't change much.

The truth, as Violet says, is that society as a whole is built on various forms of oppression, and certainly one of the most abhorrent is the one towards us women. Even without considering the right to vote, which fortunately is starting to be discussed, professions are almost inhibited for our sex, which seems destined for the home or teaching, at best. And the worst

16

part is that most of us accept this way of thinking: What would happen if battered wives rebelled? If even without reporting the incidents, since the law does not defend them, they started defending themselves, reacting, seeking revenge? Maybe I'm starting to sound like an anarchist, and it doesn't seem like the best way to think about my future marriage. But the feeling that these things will never happen to me with a man like John, while so many other women must and will face them, makes me uneasy. I can't think that these tragedies don't concern me.

London, September 19, 1888
Last night, during a moment of sweet intimacy on a walk with John, I felt compelled to ask him what the "H" stands for, the initial of his middle name, which he signs on his papers. I expected it to be the name of his father and elder brother, as is customary in many families (since I actually knew that both their names started with that letter). Instead, I was surprised when he told me with a laugh that it's Hamish, a Scottish name, chosen by his mother to honour her homeland, and which of course corresponds to James in English. How funny for an Englishman through and through like him! But the way he said it, the tenderness with which he thought of his poor mother at that moment, moved me. I squeezed his hand and promised him that from now on, when we are alone and in the sweetest moments of our lives, I would call him that. "Please call me James in those cases," he replied, laughing, "because your Scottish accent is too pure. I can't pronounce Hamish as well as you can." A little sweet secret that warms the heart of a woman who is perhaps too romantic in her heart while outwardly appearing inflexible.

London, September 30, 1888
In recent days, I have visited the glove shop where Louise works several times but have never found her. Finally, I gathered

up my courage and asked about her, only to discover that she had resigned without specifying the reason. The manager shook his head, muttering something about the fickleness of certain girls who seem to have a great need to work but then avoid the situation as if to avoid exerting themselves. It doesn't seem like a valid reason at all, based on what I have seen of this girl. I am worried: There is only one man I can turn to for advice, and I will certainly do so.

5.   Return to Baker Street

Returning to Baker Street as a customer on October 1, 1888, made quite an impression on me, although I had visited John several times before. On those occasions, the kind Mrs. Hudson never failed to offer me generous portions of her cakes, tea, and benevolence, chattering away and always concluding gleefully that she had "known from the very beginning" that I would be "a perfect wife for the doctor." This time, dismayed, she informed me that John was unfortunately not there, which I already knew because I had asked him to go out of town on an errand for me. I replied that I would wait upstairs, in the company of Mr. Holmes.

Finding myself alone with the great detective was a new situation for me. Since our first meeting, John had always been between us, like an intermediary between me and Holmes's cold and seemingly ruthless logic. Elegant and courteous as always, he put me at my ease, and from the first glance, he immediately understood that I had a problem to present to him. I explained it to him briefly. "Should we be worried?" I asked. His response was a series of questions, to which I answered as best as I could.

18

The man who argued with Louise was young, tall, and tanned. He wore a workman's shirt and a sailor's hat, both well brushed and fairly new, certainly not worn or stained. The shoes were practical and sturdy, not elegant or for evening wear. From this, I had thought that it was not a planned appointment but rather a somewhat casual encounter. He had no beard or mustache, he was cleanly shaven and his haircut was respectable. No, the man was not unkempt or disheveled. The buttons on his blouse were all in order, and a small tear on the sleeve had been duly mended. Yes, I had noticed a particular mark on the back of his left hand. From a distance, it appeared as an indistinct spot, perhaps a mole, but when the man passed by me, storming out of the park, I realized it was a tattoo: a small blue anchor.

Holmes complimented me on the accuracy of the description and the keenness of my observations. It surprised me, and it seemed like he had started looking at me with different eyes, as if seeing me for the first time.

"It is very likely that he is a sailor, and from what you say, he seems rather hot-tempered. We should try to ascertain his identity and investigate if he has been involved in any previous altercations, as is usually the case with such types," said Holmes, thinking out loud.

"If he is truly a violent man, I would be very worried about Louise's fate. I wouldn't want anything serious to happen to her."

"There's no need to jump to conclusions so quickly. However, there is indeed cause for concern. We need more information. In the meantime, if you're willing, you could ask the shop owner for an excuse to provide you with Louise's surname and address and personally verify if she is safe at home. Also, see if any of her colleagues know anything about the identity of the young sailor. As soon as you find something, come and report to me."

We bid farewell and satisfied that I was being taken seriously and excited because Holmes had made me part of the investigative process, I immediately went to the shop. There, I explained to the owner that my previous inquiries about Louise were due to the fact that the girl had promised to give me the name and address of a highly skilled and affordable dressmaker whom I urgently needed to visit to alter some clothes that were decidedly out of fashion and could no longer be worn as they were. I asked if he could recommend someone or let me speak to another saleswoman who could help me. I must have been very convincing and believable in my frivolous request, as I had become completely engrossed in playing my role, and the manager looked at me with masculine compassion and immediately directed me to a young girl who was currently free from customers.

The conversation with the girl was very fruitful. She knew nothing about the dressmaker known by Louise, but she could recommend one herself. I let her talk, took notes, and then smoothly transitioned the conversation to Louise's coworker. In short, almost without asking directly, I had all the information I needed. The sailor's name was Arnold Palmer, Louise's name was Garamond, and she lived at 47 Greenfield Road in Whitechapel.

It was late, and I had to return home, but I was so pleased with what I had discovered that I couldn't contain myself. So, I took a carriage and rushed to Baker Street. But Holmes was not there. I left him a note with the new information I had obtained and went home again by carriage, where I managed to arrive before lunch.

The next day, I went to Greenfield Road to speak with Louise. Her mother answered the door, to whom I told the same story about the dressmaker. The mother didn't seem entirely convinced, kept me at the door, and hurriedly sent me away, saying that Louise was on vacation in Edinburgh with an aunt and that she couldn't provide me with the address because, suffering from a form of nervousness, she needed rest and couldn't be disturbed. Disappointed and dissatisfied, I thought of Holmes, who had not contacted me yet, and fearing for Louise's fate, as her mother had not given me the impression of being sincere. Absentmindedly, I gave some alms to an old beggar on the street corner. Only when I checked my purse at home did I realize that I had given him a one-pound note. I was surprised at myself; it was unlike me to lose control of my behavior to that extent. The story of Louise had truly unsettled me.

I didn't know what to do. I didn't want to disturb Holmes further. If he hadn't contacted me yet, it meant that he hadn't been able to focus on my case, and I didn't think it was necessary to involve John, whom I didn't want to perceive me as a petulant and impatient girl. Perhaps I had overreacted, and my concerns were excessive.
There was nothing else to do but find out for myself. The tragedy of Pondicherry Lodge had provided me, among other things, with a measure of my courage. I had newfound confidence in myself and the strength to dare. And Holmes had further reinforced me, making me feel his esteem.

I had to find a way to approach Louise's house again without arousing suspicion. I remembered that Violet had told me about a friend from the Salvation Army. I got the address and, inventing the sad story of a brother who had died from the consequences of alcoholism, I had no trouble convincing them of my sincere interest in the movement and accompanying them on their outings to sing and preach on the streets, under the escort, of course, of a few policemen. Within a few days, I managed to join the group that sang in Whitechapel, and soon I succeeded in bringing them in front of Louise's house. I couldn't see anything strange: the windows were closed with the curtains drawn, no one entered or left. I saw that the old beggar was still there, at the corner, lying on the ground, leaning against the wall: his tattered clothes, swollen red eyes, trembling hands, and quivering voice spoke of a life of hardship and misery. I approached him to see if he had perhaps seen the girl or noticed anything strange, but to my great surprise, the old man rudely drove me away, cursing me with his hoarse voice. I rejoined the group, offended. Not that I expected special treatment for my sterling but at least a normal form of courtesy, yes. After a couple of hours of singing, as we were preparing to leave, I saw the beggar rise and, with a limping gait, approach me. He gestured for me to follow him into a dimly lit hallway. Still disturbed by his previous behavior, I hesitated until he whispered the word "Holmes." Did I hear correctly? I approached, astonished, and his eyes, which suddenly became deep and ironic, fixed on me.

"Good evening, Miss Mary," a voice I knew very well whispered to me. "We've been seeing each other quite often lately: If I told John where I found you, he wouldn't believe me."

"Mr. Holmes! I didn't recognize you at all!"

"I hope not. There are several gentlemen around here who would consider it a true honor to send me to that Creator whose praises you were singing so well just now. A good disguise is an essential passport for me in this neighborhood."

He explained that he had been there for several days for another investigation of his, regarding the Fenian terrorists, and he was surprised to see me there the first time and believed that the sterling was a sign that I had recognized him. What a high opinion he must have had of me! He added that the terrorist he was monitoring lived in the house opposite the girl's, so in the preceding days, he had also kept watch on that one once I had given him the address. Thus, he had seen Louise go out a couple of times, always accompanied by her mother, and return immediately after: she seemed to be fine, although her face was decidedly sad and downcast.

"So," I concluded, "the girl is being kept indoors to protect her from the sailor who evidently pursues her!"

Holmes shook his head.

"I can confirm that I have indeed discovered that he is a dangerous character: last year he ended up in jail for a brawl. But I have never seen him around here."

"Of course, you haven't seen him: apparently, he doesn't know where she lives, and she stays locked inside the house to ensure she can't be found!"

"Actually, if my information is correct, he should have embarked on a long voyage a couple of days ago."

"But then?"

"I haven't finished yet: an elderly man, rather badly off, has been coming in and out of that house several times in the evenings. He has an unsteady gait, is poorly dressed, and has a cough that seems to be chronic. Since I couldn't follow him, being on guard here, I had one of my Irregulars tail him. And the result is that he's the girl's father, the landlord, so to speak: a tavern-goer, a drunkard, a gambler, known to be heavily in debt."

I paused for a moment to reflect. Holmes was clearly telling me that the conclusions I had drawn were decidedly hasty.

"It seems that the picture could be different from what I had imagined. This drunken father could also be violent and responsible for Louise's bruises."

"Indeed. I still have some things to check, but we have to wait until I finish my surveillance. Come to Baker Street tomorrow afternoon. Watson will be there too, but we don't need to specify your role in this affair. It will be sufficient to tell him that you asked me to investigate the girl's disappearance."

"All right, thank you. See you tomorrow."

I quickly caught up with my colleagues from the Salvation Army, who were already walking away, and returned home, full of questions and dark forebodings.

6.   From Mary's Diary

London, October 10, 1888
The discovery that the sailor is not responsible for Louise's disappearance has left me unsettled. Could it be possible that the

bruises I saw on her were inflicted by her father? But then, why would he send her to work, presumably to squander all the girl's wages at the pub, and then confine her at home, thereby losing his source of income? And if that's the case, what role does the mother play in this matter? And why did Louise argue with the sailor? I hope that Holmes will be able to unravel this tangle tomorrow.

7.   Pest Control at Baker Street

I went to Baker Street again, and this time John was also there. Holmes had me seated, and as if he had to explain everything to me, even what I already knew, as he summarized the case. Once he reached the point I was familiar with, he continued:

"I was very interested in the man who lived right across from the Fenian terrorist and whose daughter had behaved so strangely. Since I couldn't leave, I sent Wiggins, the leader of my Irregulars, to tail him. By frequenting the same taverns as the girl's father, playing and losing at the same tables, he gradually gained his confidence to piece together the missing parts of my reconstruction of the curious incident of the girl's inexplicable dismissal."

"So, have you solved the case? Fantastic!"

"Nothing special, Watson: It was a matter of careful observation and a bit of deduction."

"So, it was the father who beat her?"

"Obviously. From the beginning, it was clear that the daughter and the wife were subjected to his violence and were victims. He would beat them and constantly threaten them with death. He had terrorized them into going to work, only to use most of the money they earned for his vices. You should have heard the chuckles with which he recounted these things to Wiggins over a mug of beer!"

"The scoundrel!"

"Unfortunately, it's an all too common story around here, Watson. But the losses had become too much, and the man had got himself into debt with a loan shark—a habitual criminal, a drug dealer, and a pimp. A despicable being, much worse than he, with a long list of misdeeds that I had sworn to make him pay for sooner or later. The old man was no longer able to pay the exorbitant interest demanded by the loan shark. He had asked for extensions several times but had already been threatened with death. Then the loan shark had a diabolical idea: He would waive the interest on the debt if the old man gave him Louise as a 'bride' — so to speak. It was then, dear Miss Mary, that I confess to having truly been horrified by human nature, though I've seen quite a lot before. That man recounted these atrocities to Wiggins with a calm air, as if it were a brilliant idea. He was almost proud to have found this way out. He behaved like a gentleman discussing his business at the club after playing billiards with another member. The girl's engagement, which was already hindered by her father who wanted her to continue working for him, had to be broken without Louise being able to resist, and she had to immediately end her employment to be at the disposal of the criminal. It was a matter of life or death for her father, you see."

That's the reason, I thought, for the argument in the park that I witnessed: Louise had broken off the engagement without an explanation. She certainly couldn't tell the truth, and the poor sailor couldn't understand why. I empathized with that poor daughter, forced through violence and blackmail to obediently follow the will of this useless, incapable, and parasitic father, to whom she probably felt inexplicably attached, as often happens to us women, and for whom she felt no responsibility for his fate. As I got lost in these reflections and wondered how we could escape from this, Holmes informed me and John of the outcome of his other investigation.

The terrorist had been arrested and swiftly convicted, thanks to the evidence that the authorities, alerted by Holmes, had found in his hideout. It included weapons and documents that Holmes knew would be discovered and for which he had personally kept watch, waiting to alert the police. Then he invited me to retire to Mrs. Hudson's rooms while he and John received Louise's father shortly after. Holmes had sent him a note summoning him to Baker Street in a peremptory manner, threatening him with grave consequences if he didn't show up.

I know that John kept his gun within reach throughout the conversation. The old man approached arrogantly and boldly, but Holmes played his cards openly: He explained that the young man to whom he had confided everything the previous evening, in his alcohol-induced haze, was his collaborator, and he presented the man with an ultimatum. Either disappear forever by boarding the first ship to the colonies and completely erasing his tracks, or meet the same fate as the loan shark, who was found with his throat cut in the middle of the street at dawn. The threat was real because Holmes had indirectly orchestrated the demise of the criminal.

The Fenians, upon learning of their leader's arrest and conviction, immediately set out to find the informant to take exemplary vengeance. It wasn't difficult for Holmes to plant some clues that incontrovertibly pointed to the loan shark. And if he had wanted, he wouldn't have had any trouble implicating the old drunkard in the affair as well, and, after all, that scoundrel deserved it. John told me that the transformation of his face was worth the price of admission to a show: From initial arrogance and rudeness, it turned into complete stupefaction as Holmes revealed how he had obtained the information about him. The color of the man's face turned a fiery red with anger, then shifted towards a greenish hue as he realized the situation, ending with a ghostly pallor accompanied by a distinct tremor, not due to alcohol withdrawal but to genuine fear.

At the end of Holmes's elucidating speech, delivered with a pipe in his mouth, calm manners, and an ironic smile, the man realized that his life hung by a thread and that he could only thank the Almighty for being offered a one-way ticket to Australia, now the only way to save his skin. He rushed off, muttering confused expressions of gratitude and bowing repeatedly.

"He'll probably get himself killed in Australia after getting involved in who knows what messes," Holmes concluded, recounting the conversation to me. Some people never change. In any case, we won't hear about him anymore."

"Thank goodness!" John chimed in, furrowing his brow and caressing my hand.

8.   From Mary's Diary

London, October 12, 1888

I hope that Louise and her mother finally find some peace, and that the girl can be reconciled with her passionate sailor. I will try to follow her discreetly from a distance, ready to intervene if needed.

I believe I have found my calling.

THE ADVENTURE OF THE REDEEMED ADDICT

1.   A Restless Night

I have more than one reason to remember well a night in April 1889, when Kate Whitney knocked desperately on our door seeking help. That poor soul shed bitter tears as she recounted to me and John the misfortune of her husband, who had fallen into the trap of opium addiction and had been missing from home for days. A pleading look from me was enough for John, as generous as ever, to put on his overcoat and rush off to a sordid opium den where that unfortunate man, according to his wife, was a regular customer and victim.

A few agonizing hours passed, during which Kate, between sobs, told me the ordeal she had endured alongside him due to his terrible condition. I tried to encourage her, accepting her horrifying confessions and occasionally offering her a bit of wine mixed with water. It was nearly midnight when we finally heard the noise of a carriage approaching in the silent street, the call of the driver, the screech of the brakes in front of our house, and finally, a discreet knock on the door. The cab driver brought the wretched Isa Whitney back home, more dead than alive but conscious: a sickly yellowish complexion, extremely pale, drooping eyelids, pupils reduced to pinpricks. He was huddled on the seat, barely able to mumble pitiful apologies to his wife.

"I didn't realize so much time had passed... There, you lose track of the hours, the days... Oh, my poor dear, I'm so sorry..."

No sign of John. The cab driver, glancing compassionately at the man he had helped to bring home, handed me a note.

"Dear Mary," it said, *"here is our friend, whom I found completely oblivious to reality in that hellish place. Unexpectedly, I encountered Holmes there, engaged in a difficult case. He asked me to accompany him, and I don't know how long I'll be away. Could you ask Anstruther to take my place? With love, John."*

I couldn't help but smile. Certainly, casually leaving a message about being absent for a few days was not exactly what one would expect from a composed professional. But I loved my husband, and I knew how much he needed the adventure that Sherlock Holmes provided him with, and how important it was to him. And I would have been truly ungrateful to protest after sending him off in the middle of the night to retrieve my friend's husband from an opium den! Yes, Isaiah and Katherine. I furrowed my brow, thinking about what lay ahead in the coming hours. The poor woman would have to face a horrible night and possibly even worse days. But certainly, the acute crisis would come immediately. The man was already starting to complain, asking for a pipe of opium. I knew what would happen, from pitiful requests to threats, maybe even violence.

"I can't leave you alone," I said decisively as she was saying goodbye and climbing into the carriage myself, I said, "I'll spend the night with you."

I won't go into the disgusting details, the tantrums, the screams, the calls for help, the agony that poor man endured in his withdrawal, and that Kate faced with determination, with my help and that of a sturdy maid who had become experienced in such situations. At dawn, I returned home, exhausted and filled with melancholy — yes, an infinite sadness had enveloped me. How can one destroy one's life and the lives of those who love you to such an extent? How can one let oneself be consumed by an abyss that drags everything deeper and deeper, without escape, toward economic ruin, social exclusion, moral destitution even before physical destitution, and ultimately death?

I managed to rest for a few hours and had just finished breakfast when I saw John arriving in a cab. He appeared fresh and rested, with a familiar sparkle in his eyes.

"Good morning, Doctor," I greeted him after kissing him. "You look satisfied, like a cat with a mouse in its mouth."

"And eager to tell how I caught it," he added.

"After you've had breakfast, John, and I'm very strict about this: You need to eat, or the entire district will criticize me for letting their esteemed doctor's physique deteriorate! Not to mention," I added mischievously, "the countless women scattered across three continents who still envy me!"

"Still with that joke? I wrote it to compliment you, after all. Don't worry about breakfast, I already ate at Baker Street."

"Which means, my dear James, that I should worry about those aforementioned women scattered, etc., etc.?"

John's joyful laughter assured me once again that his good mood could only be a sign of the success of the night's adventure. But immediately, his forehead furrowed, and he looked at me with a worried expression.

"How did it go with that wretched man?"

"As you can imagine, not well. We brought him back to his home, more dead than alive, and we watched over him all night. I managed to take over from Kate and let her rest for a few hours, although I doubt she managed to sleep, poor dear, and now he's under close supervision."

"For whatever it's worth. I've seen too many end up like that. So, you didn't sleep last night. You're truly a remarkable woman."

"Says the doctor who, after a hard day's work, first goes to retrieve a patient from an opium den in some notorious alley, and then throws himself into a mystery in the company of his detective friend! Who is more generous between the two of us, my dear? No, don't answer that. I don't know who is more generous, but I know who is more curious. If you don't tell me everything right away, I won't let you rest."

"Oh, but I slept in a real bed, and quite comfortably. Don't raise that eyebrow: I was in the company of Holmes. I slept like a log while he smoked like a Turk all night, sitting on the floor, as he does when he wants to concentrate."

"And did he solve the mystery?"

"He certainly did! Listen to this."

My husband has always had an innate ability to tell stories, which then allows him to write those magnificent stories he publishes, like *The Sign of the Four* and *A Study in Scarlet*. This talent of his gives him so much pleasure. He settled into the armchair in front of me, took hold of a pipe, calmly lit it, and with a warm smile, began smoking it and narrating, while a pleasant tobacco aroma filled the sitting room.

"I found Holmes in the opium den, disguised as an old doddering smoker" he began.

"With all due respect, it occurs to me that he didn't necessarily have to be there for an investigation," I replied.

"A wicked thought, Mrs. Watson, but I must admit it crossed my mind as well. However, the rest of the story proves that he was innocent, at least this time. A man, a gentleman who frequents the City, Neville St. Clair, has disappeared since his wife happened to see him at the window of that cursed den."

"Another victim of opium?"

"He had never shown any signs of it. When his wife saw him, he let out a scream, and someone dragged him inside. When the poor woman asked for help, and finally an officer paid attention to her, they entered that wretched place and burst into the room corresponding to the window: He wasn't there, but only Hugh Boone, a hideous-looking beggar who seems to be well-known in the City. He denied ever having seen the gentleman, but when they found the poor man's clothes in the mud of the river below the window, they took him to Bow Street, to the police station. And guess what was put inside the clothes to make them sink?"

"If you're asking me with that mocking air, it means I could never guess."

"Coins."

"That's what the beggar put inside, I bet."

"Indeed. But the poor man had disappeared and showed no sign of himself for days; that's why Holmes was in the opium den. He uncovered all sorts of illicit dealings and dreadful things and also, he told me, more than one murder. which led to the assumption that the gentleman had been eliminated. However, last night we went to see his wife, who showed us a recent note from him saying that he is alive and not to worry."

"A puzzling dilemma."

"A dilemma Holmes solved during his vigil last night. At dawn, we went to the prison, and Holmes wiped a sponge across the face of the sleeping beggar."

"A sponge?"

"With soap. Well, the beggar is the missing gentleman. Some time ago, he worked as a journalist, and to publish an investigation in his newspaper, he disguised himself as a beggar, discovering that he could earn much more that way, making funny and spicy remarks to the passersby since he is intelligent and cultured, which of course he didn't lack in his original line of work. So, dressing up as Hugh Boone, disguising his face so as not to be recognized, and spending the day on the pavement became his real occupation. When his wife saw him, he felt lost, and out of shame, he tried to hide everything. Now he has sworn to turn over a new leaf."

John then swore that I was literally left speechless hearing this story.

"Curious," I said when I regained my composure, "a story entirely based on disguises. Sherlock Holmes disguising himself in such a way and managing to infiltrate a place where many would gladly cut his throat: a gentleman who becomes a beggar, and even the arresting police officers don't realize it. It seems that disguises are essential in these matters."

"Yes, but only if done well. Holmes is a true ace: He has even fooled me more than once, coming to Baker Street disguised and inquiring about himself. Usually I mistake him for a strange visitor. He even impersonated a woman once."

"I wonder where he learned it. And where one can learn it."

"You don't need to disguise yourself, madam," John concluded, taking me in his arms, "I'm perfectly fine with you just as you are."

2.   From Mary's Diary

London, April 25, 1889
Today, poor Katherine Whitney came to visit me again, in tears. All her husband's oaths and promises were in vain. At the first opportunity she foolishly gave him, Isa disappeared for a few hours and returned with pinpoint pupils and in a state of confusion. He has resumed smoking opium just as before, and the poor thing doesn't know what to do. But something must be done:

we cannot allow this person to destroy himself without taking any action. I promised her that I would talk to John about it: He is an experienced doctor, a generous and knowledgeable man, and Katherine trusts him. Perhaps he can try to help.

London, April 26, 1889
I spent the whole night tossing and turning in bed, preparing the speech with which I would ask John for help. I immediately realized that it's not as easy as I thought: for a man of integrity and solidity like him, it is inconceivable that a person could ruin the ones they love to such an extent. His uprightness is so pronounced that he expects others to have the same purity he has always imposed on himself. I think back to the time when, despite being desperately in love with me, he managed to conceal his feelings all the while he believed me to be a wealthy heiress (or at least he tried to conceal them—it would have taken much more to hide them from a woman) because it would have been unworthy of me to marry him! So, I decided to approach the matter with caution, and at breakfast, while buttering the bread, I casually asked him what he thought of Isa and his wife's situation. He grew gloomy, and his response was blunt: He told me that as much as he, as a doctor and a man, sympathizes with him, he believes Kate should abandon him to his fate. He believes that Isa, like all addicts, is selfish and callous, and would have no qualms about harming anyone just to have his opium pipe. He also added that this is the reason he has always opposed Holmes' dependence on cocaine.

He couldn't have been clearer: I can't rely on him. Even if he were by my side, he would remain reluctant and quick to view any setbacks, even small ones, negatively. I have to think on my own. After all, in life together, in marriage, in the union of two souls, it is good for each person to have a corner of their own where they can keep their secrets, which do not necessarily have to be wicked. John has his adventures with Holmes: Why not try to do my part by fighting against evil in this sordid world that is the London we don't know, the one inhabited by outcasts, forgotten ones, and the desperate? As I wrote some time ago, I believe this is my calling, and I do not intend to give it up.

London, April 27, 1889

My plan is taking shape. To take care of Isa and Kate's case, I'll have to immerse myself in a world I practically don't know, and I must be careful not to be torn apart by the beasts like a naive animal tamer entering the cage without a clear idea. First of all, I have to do as Holmes and that gentleman did: I must be able to transform myself into another person to avoid being recognized. It requires skill, but also training.

Today, taking advantage of the hours when John is out on his visits, I went to a theatrical makeup shop that I found in the city directory, in a rather distant area of London. My heart was pounding so hard when I entered that shop! I had prepared a role to play and acted it perfectly. I was a foolish young girl, wanting to get a start as a variety actress, incredibly stupid and completely ignorant, who wanted to know how to impersonate an old woman, how to mimic wrinkles, lengthen eyelashes, and change skin color. I used a strained voice, almost shouted, interspersed with inappropriate laughter and cackles.

While the old shopkeeper passed me the tricks of the trade, I pretended not to care about what he was saying while absorbing everything attentively. One customer caught my attention, a tall woman with an interesting face and deep eyes. She, too, is an actress, she told me, with a husky and well-projected voice that must make a great impression on stage. She gave me some advice with a smile "woman to woman." She said her name was Clara Petticott. When I got home, I started practicing in front of the mirror. It's a difficult and time-consuming job, but I'll succeed.

London, April 28, 1889
I have discovered a Jewish rag dealer near Tottenham Court. It's a treasure trove of shabby and makeshift clothes, where I can find everything I need. I bought the necessary items for at least three different disguises. This morning, an old fruit vendor left my house, with a basket full of apples and a black cloth skirt like her shawl, with long hands with bluish veins. At first, I trembled at the thought that someone might recognize me, but when it seemed that everything had gone well, just near Cavendish Square, I heard someone calling me. It was Violet Forrester, who made an imperious gesture with her hand. I was paralyzed. "Good woman! I say to you, for heaven's sake! How much for an apple? I would really like one. Is five pence all right?" "Very well, Milady," I whispered, thanking her, while Violet walked away, unaware of how much I had feared being discovered, but also unaware of the immense satisfaction she had given me.

3. From Woman to Woman

In the following days after this entry in my diary, I practiced and rehearsed my different roles. Things seemed to be going well, and I had gained much more confidence in myself. On the third day, as I stepped out in the guise of the old fruit vendor, I ran into Clara Petticott, the actress I had met at the makeup shop, coming towards me with great elegance. What better test than to try before a real actress?

"Dear Lady, take one of my apples. Help a poor old woman!"

Kindly, the elegant lady turned towards me, carefully chose an apple from the basket, handed me a coin, and lowered her head towards me.

"You need to do much better than that, my dear, if you want to deceive your audience," she whispered in her husky voice. And she walked away with an ambiguous smile.

I was stunned. But she turned around and with a nod, invited me to follow her to an apartment for which she had the keys, on Regent Street. It was a luxurious and fashionable setting, with carpets, lavish curtains, and luxurious furniture.

"So, you recognized me. What a fool I've been, haven't I?"

"You didn't do badly, dear. But I have some experience in these matters, as I told you at Aaron's makeup shop. Do you want to smoke?" she commented, gracefully reclining on a sofa and taking a long pipe.

A fragrant aroma filled the room.

"Egyptian cigarettes, specially imported from Alexandria. So, here we have our little actress seeking new tricks. Forgive me, dear, but this story could have fooled poor Aaron, not an old fox like me. We are women, aren't we?"

I felt a strange sensation in front of that woman as I straightened my back again after being so hunched over. It was like a complicity, as if I could trust her.

"You're not an actress, no more than you're an old fruit vendor. Not that it scandalizes me, you know: I often pretend. What intrigues me is why you're doing it."

"Does it matter?"

"Not much, actually. But if I'm going to help you learn, I need to know whom I'm dealing with."

"Why should you help me?"

"Because I like you. And I think you like me too. Friends?"

How could I resist such disarming frankness? I told her everything, my love for John and life with him, the incident that had happened to me, the desire to help, and the idea I had to disguise myself to venture into certain environments. She listened to me gravely, nodding.

"It seems we have a female St. George on our hands. Fighting for justice and freedom, et cetera, et cetera. Noble, but quite dangerous, are you aware of that, little one? And what would your husband say?"

"Frankly, Clara, I don't think I'm doing anything wrong by trying to do my part. Ultimately, I just want to poke around a bit. But you, on the other hand, are you really an actress? This is a luxurious setting, but forgive me, I don't recall seeing your name on the billboards of the most important theaters."

The woman smiled, exhaling a voluptuous puff of bluish smoke towards the ceiling.

"Everyone has their secrets," she commented, "and it's not to say that I might share mine with you, young girl. But for now, come here and let's start with the basics. Is this the way you use the pancake makeup?"

If I had studied makeup on my own in the preceding days, from that moment on, I began attending a true makeup university, three hours a day, every day, as soon as John left for his visits. Clara taught me to change my posture, alter the color of my hair and skin, transform myself like a vaudeville artist, and within a week, she declared me a success.

"You're capable of going almost anywhere," she said after witnessing my performance as a drunken plumber. "As for your voice, remember that you had diphtheria, so you can only whisper. You can't strain your voice too much when you want to pass as a man."

"Couldn't I smoke like you, Clara?"

"I'm afraid your husband wouldn't appreciate a husky voice like mine. And besides... you and I start from very different points. You see, Mary... I'm a little ashamed I haven't told you about this yet. It feels like I'm betraying you."

Clara's expression grew serious, and I noticed her hands trembling slightly, as if she were overcome with strong emotion. She stood up, turned towards the window, and looked outside, as if she couldn't bear to meet my gaze.

"You must have figured out how I can afford an apartment of this level, and no, I'm not a famous actress."

"Who am I to judge, Clara? If you..."

"If I sell my body to wealthy men, it's my own business, isn't it? You're very generous to say that, my dear, but that's not the point. Haven't you noticed how tall I am? How large my hands are, how deep my voice?"

A slight dizziness came over me as I slowly began to understand.

"Hadn't you even considered that I might be a man? Well, now you know. Oh, a man to a certain extent, of course, a person who has never felt like one: In my heart, in my soul, in my sensitivity, I am a woman. But by law, I am called Charles. I don't want to disturb you, my dear: if you're horrified by me, I understand, I'm used to it. Don't say anything: go and reflect, if you want. Go on your search: I'll be here. If you feel like it, you can come back whenever you want to talk to me or you can choose to never cross the threshold of this house again and perhaps even shudder when you pass. Do what you feel is best."

4.   From Mary's Diary

London, May 4, 1889
After Clara's revelations, I returned home feeling quite shaken, caught in a whirlwind of emotions. But I don't have time to think about it: It's time for me to track down Isa Whitney, as I had already decided to do, and all this studying the art of disguise will serve that purpose. I told John that I would be going out for

some shopping this afternoon while he starts seeing patients in his office. I will go out dressed as a man and head to the opium den, the Bar of Gold, on Upper Swandam Lane behind London Bridge.

5.   Among Society's Outcasts

The character of the drunken plumber had worked particularly well for me, so I decided to use it again for my first official outing as a saver of lost souls. The alley was truly dark, squalid, and foul-smelling, just as John had described it, and I couldn't help but think that if I were discovered, I would have no escape amidst the degraded humanity that populated it. But I was one of them, perfectly camouflaged, and no one spared me a glance. I descended the steps that led to the opium den, opened the door, and found myself in an even darker room, unable to see the end of it due to the dense opium smoke that saturated the air.

The people, scattered on the ground without any dignity, from what little I could see, were completely lost in the sensations that the drug provided. The embers of the pipes, continually revived by the smokers, colored the atmosphere with intermittent reddish hues. I declined the pipe that the squalid individual, obviously responsible for welcoming guests, offered me and instead asked where Isaiah Whitney was, using the husky and thin voice that Clara had advised me to use. The man pointed me towards a cot at the back of the room. As I made my way towards it, I had the impression of seeing a moving shadow that had something strange about it. If it hadn't been absurd in that place, I would have said it was a child. While on one hand, I felt the need to see everything clearly, my sense of responsibility urged me to focus on my mission. I would have to clarify that matter later.

Obviously, Isa didn't recognize me, whether due to the effectiveness of my disguise or the confused state he was in, and I did nothing to make myself known. I told him that I was a friend of Dr. Watson, that he was busy with his patients, and that he had sent me to bring Isa home.

It wasn't difficult to convince him, at least, much less difficult than persuading the cab driver we stopped at the corner of the alley that we could pay for the ride, despite appearances.

Kate was stunned when she saw her husband returning home accompanied by a stranger, and her surprise was even greater when she discovered that the drunkard in front of her was me.

"What does all this mean? And where did you learn to transform like this?"

"Well, I had a good teacher, but it's a story I'll tell you another time. Now let's take care of your husband."

Once Isa was in bed, I stayed a little longer with Kate.

"Now Isa will rest, but we both know what will happen when he recovers," I told her. "And this time, you and Jane will have to handle it on your own because I want to be home before John. But Kate, dear, you can't go on like this. Drastic decisions need to be made. You can no longer trust the promises of someone who has shown that they are unable to keep them."

"What do you expect me to do? You're not suggesting that I abandon him to his fate, are you?"

"No, although I know someone who would strongly advise you to do so, for your own good. But that's not what I meant. I would like to propose that you seek help from a person from the Salvation Army who has already assisted me in the past. It's true that they deal with alcoholics, but ultimately it's about weaning him away from his addiction. I have inquired, and I know they have a residence outside London that they use for this purpose. It's expensive, not within everyone's reach, but certainly less costly than drugs. The person who needs be cured is confined there, and properly taken care of, not only for the period strictly necessary to overcome the withdrawal crisis but for as long as it takes to distance themselves from the temptation to relapse into their addiction. If you wish, you can share his seclusion, it's your choice. You need to do it immediately while you still have some influence over him and before it's too late. Tell me that you will do it; otherwise, know that I won't leave you alone anymore."

"You are so dear, Mary. All this concern for us, even though we haven't shown appreciation for your efforts and those of John. And the risks you have taken! All right, I promise that I will do everything possible to seize the opportunity you're offering me. Give me your friend's address. I will go there immediately and arrange the transfer before Isa realizes what I'm up to. Thank you, thank you. Whatever happens, I will be eternally grateful to you."

6.   From Mary's Diary

London, May 5, 1889

Last night, I managed to return home before John. I undressed quickly, removed my makeup just as fast, and hid the clothes in the trunk I designated for my disguises. But the anxiety of being discovered was overwhelming. I can't risk it like this anymore. I have decided that when I need more time for an investigation, I will invent an excuse, say that I need to travel outside London to visit a friend and won't be coming home to sleep. Of course, I'll also need to find someone who can accommodate me for the night, but I have a vague idea... as long as it aligns with his commitments...

Today, as soon as John leaves for work, I will resume my plumber disguise to return to the opium den. I want to find out if what I thought I saw is true, if that was indeed a child. If that's the case, it becomes even more imperative to get them out of that environment. I wonder, what kind of parents does a child like that have, frequenting such a filthy place?

London, May 6, 1889

It really is a child! This time, in order to observe, I had to accept - and pay for! - the opium pipe that was offered to me. I didn't inhale it, but I blew gently on it to keep it lit while hiding as best I could. After an indefinite wait, which felt eternal in my uncomfortable state, I saw him again. He wandered through the opium den, trying not to be noticed, skulking along the walls until he reached what immediately seemed to be the boss, the director, or whatever one may call the one in charge. The boss briefly lit a lamp to weigh a packet of dark powder on a postal scale, and I could see his face clearly, enough to dispel any doubt. I saw him well; he isn't a dwarf. He must be no older than 12, with red hair covered by a ragged cap, cautious yet self-assured. The two exchanged the merchandise with others whom I couldn't see clearly but who were certainly paying a substantial amount of money. In that moment, I thought the child would stop to indulge, occupying one of the cots and I was horrified. I felt a strong temptation to intervene, to shout, to do something to prevent that madness, like running out to report everything to Scotland Yard. Then I noticed that the agile little one had vanished, just as quickly as he had reached the other person. He was gone.

I rushed outside, just in time to see him sprinting towards the docks, with an obvious bulge in his jacket pocket. Where could he be going? And for whom are the drugs destined? And if I wanted to find out, how could I possibly follow him, someone so agile and fast in alleyways he knows much better than I do? I'm afraid I'll have to seek help from Sherlock Holmes and his Irregulars. I see no other way to organize a surveillance.

London, May 7, 1889
This morning, I went to Baker Street again. It's becoming almost a routine, and Holmes is no longer surprised by my visits. We haven't discussed it explicitly yet, but I'm sure he understands that my requests are not merely the result of casual observations but rather a consequence of the new activity I have seriously undertaken. And it doesn't seem to bother him; in fact, he seems to encourage me more and more, emphasizing how surprised he is by my investigative skills. And knowing that he shares affection for John, I'm certain he won't betray me by informing him

because he understands that my silence with my husband stems from my concern for his peace of mind, not a desire to keep a certain aspect of my personality hidden from him.

Mrs. Hudson, on the other hand, no longer dotes on me as she used to. I have the impression that she doesn't approve of my visits to Holmes, considering it inappropriate for a lady to regularly associate with a gentleman who isn't her lawful husband. I also think she's dying to know what we have to discuss so intimately that John isn't privy to it. I suppose it's best to let her in on the secret: I can't and don't want to make an enemy of her. She's an intelligent woman, and she'll understand.

When Holmes learned about the child's story, he agreed with me that the matter requires intervention from the authorities, but he added that to make it possible, we need to acquire more precise information. However, he strongly advised against me conducting the investigation into the boy's identity alone, and as I had hoped, he made his Irregulars available to me. They will tail him and find out where he takes the drugs and to whom, trying to learn something about his family and the motivations that have led him to involve himself in such a dangerous circle.

7.   Oliver Twist is Still Among Us

The Irregulars were, as always, efficient and punctual. It took them only two days to gather all the information Holmes and I had requested. The child, Tom Gordon, seemed to have no family anymore - assuming that was his real name and that he ever had one. He lived with three other boys of different ages in the house of an old drug addict who exploited them, taking the proceeds from their small criminal activities in exchange for a safe place to sleep and a hot meal. The rat-infested den where he

49

made them live was in a squalid alley in the docks, one of the most degraded areas of the city.

Taking advantage of the bond the boys had formed among themselves, the old man forced them to risk ending up in a workhouse or gaol by committing crimes for him. He threatened to harm the one who stayed behind while the others went to "work" if they didn't obey him blindly.

I had the information I needed. Knowing his habits and routes now, thanks to the help of the Irregulars, I intercepted Tom. This time I chose the old fruit vendor, who seemed less threatening than the drunken plumber. When I learned that he was going to replenish his supply of opium, I waited for him in the alley and stopped him just before he entered the opium den.

"Tom? Tom Gordon?" I called out to him.

"Who are you, and what do you want from me? I don't think we know each other," he replied.

"Well, you don't know me, but I know what you do and who you work for. I'm here on behalf of a very respectable gentleman who has a proposition for you."

"And who would this 'gentleman' be? What does he want from me?"

"I'm not exactly sure what he wants, but he has heard that you're someone trustworthy, and he asked me to find you. He's a gentleman, but he's a decent one."

In the end, I managed to convince him to come with me to Baker Street to speak with Sherlock Holmes. Holmes was, as always, extraordinary. Ignoring Mrs. Hudson's protests, who would never allow two types like that old lady and that rascal into the house, he made us comfortable in the study and began talking to Tom as if he were negotiating a business deal with an equal.

"Well, Gordon, you should know that I have a number of helpers who are very important for my work, which is going well. I have quite a few clients, and I need more help. I've heard that you are a trustworthy, you know how to go unnoticed and are quick at covering your tracks. What do you say to working for me?"

"But what is it about? What would I have to do? Besides, I have another job... I don't think..."

"What time is it?"

"What?"

"I asked you what time it is. You can answer by looking at one of the three watches you have in your pocket, which you must have snatched recently, likely around Regent Street, on your way to the alley where the lady found you. Probably at the corner with Piccadilly, given the type of mud on the tip of your right shoe. Come on now, quit gaping and give me an answer."

"It's... it's six o'clock, sir."

"There you go. Now, you see, I know exactly what your job is, and I inform you that you have just lost it. That old scoundrel must have been arrested ten minutes ago, if the Yard isn't running late, and he's heading to the lock-up along with the boss of that opium den he frequents. I'm well-informed; I can modestly claim some connections at Scotland Yard. And besides, it doesn't seem like that job provided you with a comfortable living arrangement.

"I'm offering you a shilling a day plus a special bonus of a guinea if you bring me, from time to time, the crucial information for solving the case. You'll have a superior to report to, named Wiggins. He'll also find you a more decent place to live than what you currently have, tell you what you are to do and receive your daily reports. We'll meet again here in two weeks and you can tell me then if you want to carry on. Of course, you can also look for another job if you like, hoping not to end up like your old boss."

"Well, I might be interested, thank you, but... I'm not alone... there are three other mates who are like brothers to me..."

"I know. Bob, Oscar, and Smithy: good lads. If they're interested too, tell them to come and meet me, and I'll propose the same conditions to them."

"But... do you know them?"

"I've observed all three of you. I never offer a job to people I don't know."

"Well, none of us noticed being observed."

"That's what happens to those whom I observe, lad."

Holmes's proposal, clear and rational without any hint of moralistic attitudes or sentimental motivations, didn't offend Tom's pride. It convinced him to enlist himself and recruit his friends into the Irregulars. As Holmes had predicted, the old man ended up in jail, reported by the detective for fencing stolen goods, theft, and organizing a gang of young delinquents under his command. The police never managed to uncover the names of the boys involved.

The vile opium den was temporarily closed, and the owner was sentenced to ten years following an investigation in which Holmes demonstrated that several bodies had been silently disposed of in the Thames through a trapdoor in that establishment. Inspector Lestrade was astounded by the evidence of that crime, based on the analysis of wood splinters found beneath the skin of some of the corpses. Holmes congratulated me for the way I had conducted the operation, pleased that I hadn't taken unnecessary risks and had listened to his recommendations.

8.   From Mary's Diary

London, May 12, 1889
Tom Gordon has been rescued from the squalid and hopeless life to which he seemed condemned, and along with him, his three friends as well. When Tom accepted Holmes's offer, they bid farewell with a handshake, like two business partners, but I could see, in both their eyes, the glimmer of an emotion that united them, even if neither wanted to let it show. Perhaps it was a small thing, but tonight I feel happy for having turned an inhuman and certainly fatal experience into a potential life of dignity.

TWO DROPS IN THE OCEAN

1.   A Special Friend

Helen Barrister was one of my first London friendships: I met her after I had been welcomed into the Forrester household upon leaving the institute in Edinburgh, while accompanying the children one day to soak up some sun in the park. I was struck by that tiny person, with such a refined but unhappy air, who always read alone for hours on a bench; I understood the reason for that sadness and loneliness when she stood up to limp back home, due to a deformed foot that almost certainly had afflicted her from birth. From that day on, I had made a commitment to sit next to her whenever I should meet her again, and so I did: A delicate friendship was born between a wounded and frightened person of the world and a young woman who was also scared but fascinated by the great risks and opportunities of the metropolis. After my marriage she began to visit me from time to time, to talk about literature and poetry, especially since she had read my husband's books and admired his writing skills. One afternoon, while we were having tea and chatting, I noticed a melancholic tone that I hadn't noticed in her since, thanks to our friendship, she felt less alone.

"Why do you avoid my gaze, dear?" I began.

"But you're mistaken, Mary, really."

"What troubles you? Don't lie to me, please. You can't even keep your hands still from your nervousness. Our friendship is too close for you not to confide in me, don't you think?"

A deep sigh marked her surrender after a long silence that revealed an inner conflict. Finally, she reached out and took my hands in hers, while a veil of tears moistened her eyes.

"Forgive me for lying, Mary. It's just that I didn't want to trouble you with my silly anxieties. You're married now, living with that wonderful man, and you should enjoy your happiness. It's not right for me to distress you with the whims of my lonely life, knowing well that I'll remain alone for the rest of my life. No, it's not right."

"What nonsense! And now that you've brought up the absurd reasons that led you to hide from your friend what torments you, would you please stop being foolish and tell me everything from the beginning, without wasting any more time?"

"Oh, dear Mary," she said, clapping her hands in amusement amidst tears, "isn't that how Mr. Holmes always says it, according to your husband's books? To tell everything from the beginning? Will you also light a pipe now, scrutinizing me closely?"

We burst into laughter, and Heaven knows we needed it. Little Helen seemed like a wet chick at that moment, evoking a feeling of sympathy and protection that reminded me of times gone by: That poor girl had a desperate need to uplift her spirits. So, I rushed to John's desk, grabbed one of his pipes, and put it in my mouth, sitting in front of her with a serious air.

"Tell me everything, Miss Barrister," I insisted.

It took her a while to stop laughing, but that curious interlude helped her open up without hesitation.

"You know that I have been living with my brother, Philip, since our parents died many years ago. We are not rich, but the small inheritance our parents left us, together with what he earns from his work, is more than enough to live a peaceful and trouble-free life. Philip is my whole life, along with the few friendships I have cultivated over the years - yours being the most important – and reading, and tending to my flowers in our small garden."

"I know you spend a lot of time alone."

"But I'm not bored, you know? Philip has his job, which may not be very satisfying, but it pays well. He works for Mr. Jones in Clerkenwell, a pawnbroker agency, but a very reputable one, nothing to do with swindlers or loan sharks. My brother tells me there are many shady characters in that world, but luckily Mr. Jones is an upright and courteous person, and Philip has always been pleased to work there."

"Your brother, from what I know of him, seems to be of unwavering moral rectitude."

"Exactly. Perhaps too much at times. I hear him making very sharp comments about the ladies he knows or encounters in his work. Frankly, I find them a bit excessive, extreme. I'm starting to think he's about to embrace the Presbyterian confession, you know? You knew it well up in Edinburgh..."

"Yes, indeed, it's the predominant church in Scotland. Very good people, but a bit too rigid perhaps. But is that what troubles you so much?"

"No, of course not. The thing is, Philip is changing. For weeks now, I've seen him distracted, absent-minded. During dinner, I talk to him about what I did during the day, and he smiles at me with a vacant look and gazes out the window. Occasionally, I ask him a trick question, and I realize he hasn't even been listening to me. There's something bothering him."

"Forgive me, but perhaps he's in love?"

"Oh, I should wish to Heaven he were. I would be so happy for him! I thought about it, and I was almost certain when I found traces of lipstick on his handkerchief. But he vehemently denied it when I told him, and please believe me, I said it with a smile, congratulating him. He explained that a lady felt ill at the shop, and he revived her by spraying water on her face. He lent her his handkerchief to dry herself, and that's how the stain happened."

"It is indeed possible that it happened that way."

"Certainly, but then why is he so distracted? What troubles him? And where does he go at night?"

"At night?!"

"We have dinner quite early, and we retire to our rooms no later than nine. Last week, there was a heavy storm, and one thunderclap was louder than the others, waking me up around midnight."

"I remember. It was a dreadful night. The thunder was incredibly loud, and the wind in the park knocked down several trees."

"Exactly. Suddenly awakened, with the rain drumming on the windows as if it were about to shatter them, thunderclaps making me jump, flashes of lightning illuminating the house... I'm not easily frightened, but that was too much even for me. With my heart in my throat, I got up and went to get some water, wandering around the house trying to calm down. It must have been midnight, and what a surprise it was to see the door open silently and my brother tiptoeing in, fully dressed though shabbily and drenched in water."

"Did you ask him where he had been?"

"Certainly, and that's when things got even stranger. He didn't expect to find me awake and apologized profusely for scaring me like that. He said that because of the storm, he had gotten up to check if there had been any damage in the neighborhood, taking a quick stroll down the street. I pretended to believe him, but Mary, it wasn't true. He must have been outside for quite some time to get that wet. So, being suspicious, I stayed awake the following nights to see what was happening. I discovered that almost every evening, my brother dresses up and sneaks out around ten, only to return in the dead of night, sometimes much later than that stormy night. Now, what would your friend Holmes say about this strange case?"

"He wouldn't say anything," I replied, shaking my head, "without sufficient information. I believe he would further investigate. Nevertheless, I don't think there's a real crime involved."

"May Heaven protect us, Mary, I don't think so either. But put it all together: the nightly outings, my brother's obvious distraction and worry, his unusual silence with me about what's happening to him. It distresses me greatly. And add to that the fact that his wallet is always empty. Yes, forgive me, I snooped. Where does he keep his small savings that he used to use for occasional little gifts to cheer me up?"

I tried to comfort the poor woman as best I could, and when she left, she seemed more at ease, perhaps also due to the generous amount of apricot cake she had consumed. I don't believe there is a worry in the world that can withstand three slices of Mrs. Hudson's famous apricot cake from Baker Street, which she insists on supplying me with regularly, firmly believing that it will uplift my spirits and help me conceive little Watsons soon.

2.   From Mary's Diary

London, May 25, 1889
From everything that has happened recently, I have drawn several lessons, all fundamental. It's strange how a grown woman, already married, can discover how much there is to learn: I would never have imagined that one day I would find myself pretending to be someone else, and I smile at the thought of the horror that would engulf my good teachers in Edinburgh if they knew what I have been up to. And who knows what John himself would think, as he knows the world of the poor and those who live beyond the boundary that separates good society from outcasts better than I do. Yet I have learned that one thing is to consider that world with attention, with kindness, even with condescension, and another is to try to understand it: to truly make an effort to change the destinies of those involved. To the

extent that I can, that is: It is not in my nature to join great movements in an attempt to overthrow the established order and promulgate new and different rules. I'm not even sure if those wouldn't create other distinctions, other boundaries, and certainly, in any case, I am not cut out for that kind of activity. More modestly, I would like to do something for those in need, but to do so, I know that I can't simply observe from a distance, I have to immerse myself in that world. And so, I must continue to move within it, and talk and discuss with those who are part of it. To start, it is time to return to Clara - and soon.

London, May 26, 1889

Said and done. I knocked with some trepidation and a pounding heart. How would she receive me? When she confessed her secret to me, she expected me to come forward, and I feared that perhaps I had taken too long, leaving her to think that I despised her, that I was horrified by her way of being and her way of living. But as soon as she opened the door, all my fears vanished: She lit up with a radiant smile, happy beyond any doubt. She confessed to me later that she was afraid she would never see me again, and the fact that I accept her for who she is, without judgment, seems to her an extraordinary gesture coming from a married woman of good society. To me, frankly, it doesn't seem so, and I told her that. Conventions are just deeply ingrained habits, and if I have learned anything since I was a child, it was that people should be understood and loved, never judged. Imagine if I should start doing that now.

"Yes. At your venerable age," she said, and we laughed like two girls.

I told her about what is happening to me: How the matter of the Whitneys ended and how I realized that beneath the surface of society, there is a world of suffering and terror. It is not human to turn away and think of other things. Clara, looking at me with compassion, once again compared me to a knight-errant, casting doubt on the possibility for anyone to truly change things, but I insisted that I will do what little I can. Someone else will take care of the rest. After all, my husband takes care of people who fall ill because they all live in desperate hygienic conditions. It is evident that the situation should be changed, but for now, he saves the lives of those he can. And it is not just a job, it is his way of life and thinking. I want to do the same, in my own small way: not saving lives, not solving mysteries like his friend Holmes, but at least lending a hand, yes. And since I need to know the world I want to help, I need Clara's help, and I asked her for it.

We discussed things for a long time. She has already taught me almost everything she knows about the art of disguise and makeup, although she confessed that she still keeps some personal secrets to herself. But what I'm asking her for is full support: a place in the city where I can change without leaving and returning home with the nightmare of encountering John. Perhaps, if necessary, a place to sleep if I were forced to be away from home for a few days with an excuse to tell my husband. Yes, my husband. Of this new life, of these adventures that happen to me, this is the only thing that weighs on me, having to lie to John. But I must protect him in some way: he would not tolerate the idea that his wife is not at home, safe, but wandering in the city at the risk of getting into trouble. John is a terribly sensitive person, already too wounded by life to bear the anxiety I would cause him.

In the end, Clara enthusiastically agreed to the plan. She says she feels a bit like Saint George herself, lending me a hand!

Now I have the keys to her house, which will be my base for my adventures in the realm of the unknown. She recommended that I enter and exit through the service entrance because her address is well-known in certain circles, and someone might notice a young woman entering a house that is, let's say, talked about. Perhaps her scruples are excessive, but if I have learned anything from what John told me about his friend Holmes, covering one's tracks is very important. He told me that the great detective has never appeared in a newspaper portrait, and no one - except those who know him personally - knows what he looks like.

London, May 27, 1889
I didn't even have time to secure a safe refuge where I could disguise myself and move freely in London without arousing John's suspicion when my husband discovered that I was acting behind his back.

This morning, John informed me that he would accompany Holmes to Italy, where he would stay for a few days on an important mission, about which he couldn't provide further details. It must be something secret related to the government: Holmes is no stranger to such commitments.

I told him that I would also be away for a while, needing to spend some time in Bath with a relative who had broken her leg and needed assistance. After muttering a few remarks about how I am like a beacon attracting all souls in need of comfort, John kissed me, giving the customary recommendations. I also advised him not to take excessive risks, knowing well that anything can happen with Holmes, and he left to go to Waterloo Station.

I packed a bag for a few days, intending to send a porter to pick up my trunk of disguises the next morning, seizing the unexpected opportunity of John's prolonged absence for an operation that would have been more complicated to carry out with him around. Then I hurried out, but before going to Clara's, I thought I would stop by Cardinal Newport's, who has been so close to me in my work with the poor and the disenfranchised, to inform him that I had found a way to evade John's control and, consequently, dedicate myself more freely to the cause.

As I was leaving Cardinal Newport's study, while bidding him farewell, John appeared at the door. We were both stunned. What was he doing there? Wasn't he supposed to be at the station? After saying something in a low voice to Newport, John said his goodbyes and, taking me by the arm, forcibly brought me to an empty sitting room. There, he demanded an explanation for my presence in that building. I could do nothing but confess part of the truth, the part regarding my support for the social initiatives of the Catholic Church, explaining that I had lied to him only to avoid worrying him, still expecting an angry reaction from him. However, as always, John proved to be the best of men because not only did he forgive me, but he showed understanding for the reasons why, like him, I am willing to take risks in the name of a higher ideal. I kissed him and flew off to Clara's house.

3.   On the hunt

On Wednesday afternoon, I stepped out of Clara's back door dressed as a man, perhaps a bit short, but with a grim face and a scar on my left cheek. Not a sailor, as I had hoped, because Clara dashed my enthusiasm with a single phrase: "Where are the

63

calluses on your hands?" Nonetheless, my worker with a troubled past was entirely believable.

I had also learned to smoke, which allowed me to loiter nonchalantly near Helen's house until I saw her brother Philip come out. He was a handsome young man, tall and distinguished, but strangely dressed in a shabby manner. Where could he be going at that hour with unpressed trousers and a coat that had almost lost its original color, I wondered? Not to mention the crumpled worker's cap he had stuffed in his pocket who knows how many times. A woman notices such things, and I thought I couldn't understand how Helen had suspected a female presence in her brother's life.

A light fog had descended on the streets, and it wasn't difficult to follow him, keeping my distance as he walked under the yellowish puddles of lamplight. But soon he veered into narrower, less crowded streets, and I had to get closer to keep him in sight. I had lost my sense of direction almost completely, and all I knew was that we were getting closer and closer to areas I wasn't familiar with, venturing into the East End between Whitechapel and Stepney: places where a respectable young lady would never walk alone during the day, let alone at that hour. Should I continue? But then, how could I possibly turn back, to where? I shuddered once again and continued to follow him.

The distant source of light that suddenly appeared in the darkness of those alleys was a pub with an ambiguous name, "The Wobbling Goose," into which Philip plunged while two stumbling drunks stumbled out into the mud of the alley. Inside, it was chaos. The air was so thick with smoke, steam, and the burnt oil of lamps that at first, it prevented me from seeing what was in front of my eyes. Men drank, shouted, laughed, while others played cards and blasphemed in a way that, I couldn't help but think, would horrify my Salvation Army friend to the core.

Scantily clad women roamed among the customers, sitting beside them, often on their laps, laughing and screaming even louder than the men, inviting them to follow them upstairs. In one corner, an old Irishman played the fiddle next to another man playing the accordion as fast as he could, on a devilish tune I didn't know and that seemed more desperate than cheerful, while all those people fidgeted, laughed uproariously, drank, smoked, shouted, and occasionally ended up in a brawl, immediately stopped by two or three brutes who must have been in the employ of the pub's owners. I tried to remain impassive, true to my disreputable character, and got myself a beer, settling in a corner to observe what was happening, and above all, trying not to lose sight of Philip. What was that Presbyterian lad doing in a place like this? The boy didn't seem too uncomfortable in the place he clearly knew well: He exchanged greetings with a couple of unsavory characters who responded, and he looked around anxiously.

"Good evening, handsome lad. Feeling lonely, huh, cutie? My name is Dolly. You'll buy me a drink, won't you?!"

I almost jumped out of my seat when I saw that a woman just a little older than I, already too old for the profession she was in, had sat down next to me with a suggestive air. Her dress and low neckline left little to the imagination, her heavy breath and vacant eyes betrayed what she must have drunk and smoked until that moment. I gave her a faint smile and passed my mug to her with a brisk gesture.

"I've got few pennies tonight, sweetheart," I said in the hoarsest voice I could muster, "but you can drink if you want. For the rest, I'll have to wait until tomorrow: I'll come back to see you with some money."

"I'm counting on it, beauty," she replied, already disinterested. But she still couldn't resist the beer, poor woman. "I've never seen you around here, you're new."

"I'm not from London, I come from Richmond. I came to work with Philip."

"Philip?"

"That guy over there."

"Ah, I see. Violet the Red's man. She calls him Pip."

At that moment, Philip lit up as from upstairs appeared what I immediately recognized as Violet the Red. Beautiful, radiant, an angelic face with two enormous green eyes beneath a crown of fiery red curls. A grace and elegance in her movements that were entirely unexpected in such a dump, where the girls staggered under the influence of absinthe and opium, blasphemies resounded at every table, and noise drowned out everything. Yet, in that sort of infernal circle, her appearance seemed to split time in two, as if an angel had appeared out of nowhere, wiping away all the chaos and ugliness that surrounded her. The flashy dress, the ghastly taste of the low-cut corset and excessive necklaces she wore didn't matter. She emitted a ray of light and beauty, amidst the sewer and decay.

"Isn't she beautiful, right?" my new friend said, noticing my gaze. "Tell me, did you lie to me? Do you have the money? But it's useless for you to think about

Violet; she's in love, you know. She's with Pip. At least when Pip is here."

"What are you saying?" I reproached her, pushing her slightly. "What do I care about your redhead? And I told you I don't have money. But maybe I have just enough for another beer if you want. Tell me about Pip."

It didn't take much to get her talking, while I observed Philip and his Violet sneaking away and locking eyes, smiling. That place belonged to Sam, a well-known man in the neighborhood, and many were even afraid to utter his name, Sam. My new friend didn't hesitate to speak about him because she had been a dear friend of Sam's a while back. I understood, you see, what she meant. Sam would never harm her. Of course, one had to have respect for Sam, a lot of respect. Violet was his new woman, the one he frequented the most.

"I don't understand, darling. Didn't you say Violet is Pip's girlfriend?"

The woman almost choked with laughter, bursting out while finishing her beer, and it took her a while to recover.

"You're such a child, boy! But here, aren't we all in the same business? Violet is Sam's woman, but she also has to work and earn him money. But she's also his woman when he wants her. And now Sam wants her to keep Pip on a hook. But why do you care so much about all this, huh?"

I changed the subject before she could get suspicious, telling her that I didn't care at all about Violet or Pip, after all. But I liked that place, and I saw so many beautiful girls, like her, and many good people. It was a classy place, that's what it seemed like to me, really top-notch. Of course, there was that girl behind the counter, black as ebony, who seemed out of place. What was that kind of child doing there? Washing dishes?

"She's too young to earn a living like us. Sam picked her up from the streets years ago and put her to work behind the counter, cleaning and tidying up. But now she's about to make the big leap."

"What leap?"

"She's just become a woman... you know what I mean. So there will be an auction for her: She may not be a great beauty, but she's black, and the exotic always sells. I remember a Chinese girl who caused a sensation. The highest bidder will be the first to taste her, you see? Many others have gone through this before her. And in the end, it has to come to this. After all, Sammy might as well recoup the money he spent to support her. Listen, though, beauty, if you really don't have money, it's better for me to chat with someone else. I need to earn something too, don't you know? Thanks for the beer, and see you tomorrow. I'll be waiting."

And she sauntered provocatively through the hall, looking for other customers.

When I returned, at an unbelievable hour, to Clara's house, there was still music and lights in the parlor. I didn't approach for obvious reasons and went straight to my room, but I had difficulty falling asleep. Too many things, too many ugly things.

4. The Penang Lawyer

The next morning, during breakfast, I couldn't hold it any longer and told Clara everything. She listened to me patiently, with sorrowful eyes.

"Even worse things happen beneath the surface of this peaceful society."

"I can imagine. But this is happening right in front of me. Is it possible that nothing can be done?"

"The law certainly can't intervene, assuming anyone would even care."

"That's what hurts me the most."

I explained that I had managed to speak to her, I approached the girl that everyone usually ignored and started asking her a few things. She was a very beautiful girl: fine regular features, coal-black eyes, intelligent and lively, and with flawless skin, her hair styled in African braids that reached down to her shoulders. She was quiet, polite, and seemed quite happy. I cautiously asked her about her life, her hopes, and what truly horrified me, I explained to Clara, was that she seemed completely calm about what was about to happen to her, and it all seemed perfectly normal to her. She agreed to be sold like a slaughterhouse animal.

"You see her as you are, a good person and a respectable bourgeois. But that's not the perspective of the girl and those who live like her."

"What do you mean?! Do you think what's going to happen to her is right?"

"That's not the point. The fact is, there's no alternative in that world. The girl would have died of hardship years ago if Sam hadn't taken her in, only to subject her to the fate she's facing now. You sympathize with one child, not with all the other girls surrounding her in that place and in the neighborhood..." she said. Then she suddenly fell silent.

"You left the conversation unfinished."

"...However, it's better to do something than nothing. I came up with a rather amusing idea, but I won't tell you a word until tonight. Get ready to go out later. After all, I'm not a weakling..."

"But you would like to be one!" I commented playfully, and we burst into laughter.

At exactly ten o'clock, Clara's appointment house unexpectedly closed its doors: no music, no lights. She had arranged to meet me in the entrance hall, and I can't describe my surprise when I saw Charles descending the staircase instead of Clara, wearing a perfect evening dress and holding a Malacca cane, with a radiant smile illuminating his face.

"You look wonderful, Clara... or Charles? How should I address you?"

"In the masculine, tonight. I'm on a mission. Well, what do you think? Not bad, huh?"

"A true waste, no doubt."

"You shameless girl! I remind you that you're a married woman. Now let's focus on you. You're too 'goody-goody,' and this will be your trial by fire."

"What do you mean?"

"That tonight, you'll portray something that's completely opposite to you, your way of being, your way of feeling. You'll have to be a great actress."

"Don't tell me..."

"Exactly! Tonight, you'll be like me: a woman of the night. I can't show up at that auction without an adequate presentation. A beautiful, eye-catching high-class prostitute by my side will be my business card and make my charade much more believable."

Clara gave me a dress suitable for the character I had to play, probably borrowed from a friend of my size. It was so tight at the waist that it almost burst my bosom, and it was much more revealing than anything I had ever worn in my life. Dizzying slits in the skirt showed my legs, sheathed in fishnet stockings, ending in improbable black pointed boots with high heels. The makeup, very conspicuous, was personally done by my friend and was so effective in overloading all my features that I had a hard time recognizing myself in the mirror. However, the most difficult part was being believable in those clothes because I couldn't find any inner resonance in them. Just as Clara had predicted.

Then I had an intuition: I would lean on her image, imitate her to the point of parody. If she were believable, so would I be. In the worst-case scenario, I told myself, they would mistake me for a man in disguise. Arriving in my friend's private carriage and stepping out in all my finery in the dirty square near the establishment I had visited the previous evening caused a stir among the local population. They approached us with suspicion and evident interest in my preux chevalier's watch, wallet, and my purse. But the situation cleared up immediately when it became evident from the facts that Clara's stick was reinforced with lead and its owner knew how to use it very well. The news that two ruffians had limped away and another scoundrel had a bloody head quickly spread through the street and the venue, and when we entered the crowd, no one even thought of giving us the slightest trouble.

"You're skilled with that stick too," I commented.

"Yes, I've managed to get by in my time. 'Lawyers' like this one are capable of convincing even the toughest heads of the error of their ways" [1] said 'Charles,' proudly showing his weapon. "Wait, look, that must be the famous Violet the Red. And your friend Pip, from what I can see," he added.

I could see them too, sitting at a slightly secluded table in a corner. She was all sweet cooing, and he was literally lost in her eyes.

"He handed her something."

"Yes, I saw it. And she seems extremely grateful to him. That's your little black doll, instead. It seems like quite a grand evening."

Indeed, the black girl was dressed up like a little woman. Her lips were covered with vibrant red lipstick, and garish makeup marred her features. She wore a corset so tight that it accentuated her small breasts, and her skirt revealed a high slit on

---

[1]   It is the reason why Malacca canes were also known as "Penang lawyers".

one side. The whole ensemble seemed simultaneously repulsive and fascinating in its horror.

"The person who dressed her like that deserves to be in jail for bad taste," remarked my friend acidly.

"Well, the person who dressed me isn't any better," I added ironically.

"There is a difference: Despite the vulgarity of your appearance and despite your efforts to get into character, you maintain an undeniable underlying dignity, which makes you both irresistible and unattainable. In fact, maybe even more irresistible because you are evidently unattainable. Even I wouldn't be able to resist your charm... But that poor girl, beneath the disguise, all that remains is sad bewilderment."

I had already sensed that Clara, beneath her apparent cynicism, concealed a profound sensitivity, perhaps the fruit of painful past experiences, and I was happy to share with her the unease that the ugly business had stirred in both of us.

The atmosphere around us was becoming frenetic, much like the previous evening. The women, almost as drunk as the men, were jumping from one man's lap to another, and slaps and laughter filled the air. Beer flowed abundantly, and the music grew increasingly frantic. The audience seemed partially different from the previous night, I noticed: workers and common folk, but also respectable bourgeoisie. And someone as elegant as my friend roamed among the crowd, casting glances at the black girl. Someone even tried to approach her as if wanting to ensure the quality of the product, but they were prevented at the last moment by a couple of brutes positioned at her sides.

At one point, a gong sounded, paralyzing everyone and capturing their attention. A massive man, with a vulgar face and a pair of hideous red sideburns, emerged from behind a curtain and stood next to the girl. His pig-like and cruel eyes, his lips tightened like an assassin, and his malicious, icy voice immediately made me understand that he was the infamous Sam, the owner of the establishment and undisputed boss of the neighborhood. With a falsely ceremonious air, he began to explain why the evening was particularly special and why the honored guests and friends should be interested.

The little Amina was no longer so little, that was the point, and we were all there to witness her initiation into the world of respectable adult men and women. Therefore, following the house tradition, the auction for the first night of the African Princess, the Black Panther of Whitechapel, which would drive the men of London mad for years to come, was now open.

I looked at that poor girl, and it felt like I was living in a nightmare: she seemed frightened now, and I noticed that she was trembling slightly behind a forced smile. But this seemed to excite the men around me even more, instead of irking them like it did me, and soon someone started shouting his bid, and the price began to rise. The regular patrons of the establishment were quickly excluded from the bidding in favor of the wealthy customers who had come for the occasion, which caused a certain murmur of disapproval that was promptly silenced by the owner, who watched with satisfaction as his profits grew.

"Two pounds!" shouted an elderly gentleman to my right.

"Two and a half!" replied an elegant gentleman at the back of the room. And then there was a rather long silence.

"One hundred guineas," I heard a confident voice next to me.

Charles stood up with a bored expression and calmly walked towards Sam, positioning himself in front of him as if admiring paintings in a museum.

"One h..."

"One hundred, yes. But not for just one night, my good man: I'm buying her in bulk. I'm taking her away."

The owner licked his lips as a subdued murmur testified to the astonishment of the crowd.

"But why?"

"Stupid question. It's my business. Anyway, I plan to establish a high-class brothel down in Westminster, nothing like this place, no offense. And the black girl seems like a good deal to me. As for you, my friend, aside from tonight, you won't be able to demand much for her anymore, and soon she'll lose all her value. Considering that you feed her, she won't earn you more than ten or twenty guineas a year, and for a year or two at most. It's in your best interest, isn't it?"

The owner seemed undecided, evidently caught off guard by an offer he didn't expect. Then a cunning smile seemed to appear on his ugly face, and at his signal, the brutes moved threateningly towards Charles. It happened in an instant: the cane swung in the air, and the two thugs fell to the ground with bruised heads, while Sam found himself with his arm bent behind his back and a sharp knife pointed at his throat.

"Bad move. But I forgive you. You thought I had money in my pocket and you thought you could pull off the heist. But it's going to cost you: We're at sixty pounds now."

"But how?!"

"Fifty, final offer. And, as you can see, the knife is already sinking into your flesh. Do you agree or will your girls have to clean the floor? Blood stains."

"All right... all right."

"You'll accompany me outside, along with the girl and my friend. One last thing," he added, whispering in his ear, "You're known around here, but I have friends everywhere. If you so much as think about getting revenge, your corpse will be floating in the river within a few hours. I've taken care of many like you, and I haven't regretted it at all. Now let's go, you blockhead."

I took the girl's hand, and we walked out. At the corner, the carriage was waiting for us.

5.   Breakfast at Clara's

At breakfast, for the first time, there were three of us: the two of us and Amina. The young girl was naturally a bit bewildered by everything that had happened to her and the sudden change in her life that had occurred in a few hours. She was certainly surprised, after being taken away the previous evening by a couple, to find herself having breakfast with two women, to begin with. But it was the whole new world she had ended up in that must have astounded her. And, as Clara expected, she wasn't quite happy with the change: The future of being a prostitute, however ugly, was a future she knew well, but what would this new life hold for her? What price would she have to pay for the comfort and luxury surrounding her?

By asking the right questions and approaching her with tact, however, we had no trouble getting her to tell us her story and everything we wanted to know about Sam's establishment and Violet the Red. Amina told us she was the daughter of a poor black girl, who was also a prostitute and had died at a young age, and that she had spent all her years in Sam's brothel. She spoke of it as a normal place, sufficiently warm in winter and with enough food to sustain oneself. She didn't ask for anything more, nor did she receive anything else. She said she had no regrets, although she admitted she had taught herself to read from the newspapers she happened to glimpse, and she would have loved to play the violin like Billy the Irishman.

"What can you tell us about Pip and Violet the Red?"

"What you would expect. He was a regular customer at Sam's for many years: he would come occasionally, spend a few hours with a girl, and leave. But he fell head over heels for Violet."

"Are you sure?"

"Violet knows how to work her magic, she's good. In the end, she fed him the same story, that she's in love with him but can't leave the establishment or Sam would kill her."

"Indeed. The only way to save her is to give Sam a lot of money, right? So that he lets her go free. That's why Philip doesn't have a penny left."

Amina nodded, in a serious manner: She must have witnessed such scenes many times and it probably didn't shock her as much as it would shock me to see a fish caught on a hook. But in her little face, I saw an uneasiness that I understood, but it struck me.

"I... I would like to ask something," she timidly began. "I saw that the gentleman... I mean... the lady bought me. Will I have to please other men... or women?"

"Dear, forget what I said last night," Clara replied calmly. "Certainly, this house has its peculiarities, and I am the epitome of it: I imagine you won't be scandalized by so little. I only ask you not to pay attention to what happens here in the evenings. You won't have to do anything except go to bed early in your own room."

"But I cost fifty pounds! It's an enormous sum."

"It's an investment. You seem intelligent, and you said you would like to read and study. Now, I need a good lawyer to protect the business of the house. Disguising oneself for the law is not a crime, as it is considered a kind of joke. Sodomy is another matter, but it needs to be proven, which is not easy if you have a good lawyer: You will study law and repay me with interest."

"Clara! A female lawyer?! A black one, moreover?"

"Oh, how times change. In Canada, they have been fighting for female lawyers for a long time, and even if it's taking longer here, I just need a capable girl who studies cases and outwits the pompous lawyers at the Temple to say what I want: a behind-the-scenes job. It's not that I lack lawyer clients, but I would feel more secure having someone I can trust to give me their opinions. Is that all right with you, Amina?"

"For me, it's a dream," she replied, her eyes widening. And I saw her smile for the first time.

"Now, dear, go over there, please. The two of us need to discuss our matters."

We sat there, alone at the table, thinking and reflecting on everything that had happened. Clara gazed at the ceiling with half-closed eyes; the cigarette in her mouth emitted small bluish puffs that rose steadily upwards. From the street below, the normal noise of traffic, carriages, curses of the coachmen, the mischief of the urchins, and the regular footsteps of people bustling through the streets of the metropolis could be heard. Clara broke our silence with a sigh and a cryptic comment.

"Interesting."

"What's interesting, excuse me?"

"That you behave exactly like your husband. You tend to throw yourself headlong into adventures and appreciate the romantic aspects of the case, the emotional details, but instead of presenting the facts for what they are and letting the listener put them in the right logical order - at least according to what Holmes says in your husband's books. And, moreover," she hurriedly added, seeing my raised eyebrows, "like your husband, you also have the rare gift of remaining silent without asking questions until the opportune moment."

"Which would be now."

"Exactly. I must say, though, you have shown quite a bit of courage and even recklessness, if you allow me, by joining me, dressed the way you were, in Sam's pub in Whitechapel. That man is much more dangerous than you think, and several bodies slipped into the Thames could testify to that, if only they could speak."

"So you think we should fear retaliation?" I replied, concerned.

"And, like Watson, you worry about your friends and not yourself. No, I don't think you, me, or Amina has anything to fear. In the end, Sam made a great deal, and he has already realized what a tough nut I am to crack, almost like smashing one's teeth."

"All's well that ends well."

"But not everything has ended well yet, which brings us to our problem. Excellent work, yes. But the issue of your friend's brother is not resolved yet: The case is not closed."

Indeed, that was the case, and I had been thinking about it all night.

"I think I understand how he could have lost his head like that, Clara. That man has made a tough life choice. Don't give me that ironic expression: have you ever wondered why a handsome young man like him never fell in love before?"

"Because of Helen?"

"Exactly," I said, getting up and pacing back and forth in the living room, waving a cigarette between my fingers. "He loves his sister, he knows very well that under the circumstances she's in, it will be impossible for her to marry or even find someone who will fall in love with her. So he decided to stay by her side and never fall in love himself. That's why he's so rigid when it comes to the women his sister timidly proposes, that's why he appears like a 'Presbyterian.' He has decided to completely and harshly suppress his emotional side, only indulging in occasional relationships with street girls. I wonder how this Violet managed to penetrate that armor... but she did, and he collapsed with all his morals. He would do anything for that woman."

"Perhaps if you spoke to him frankly..."

"Oh, dear Clara, let me tell you that there's no opening in that direction. If men were logical or reasonable in their affairs, they would behave very differently, believe me. I wouldn't achieve anything: he might listen to me patiently all the way through, in the name of the friendship between me and his sister, but he would say that I'm wrong."

"But what reason would you have for saying these things?"

"Because I'm a woman, and I make things up."

"But Amina could testify!"

"An unreliable testimony: Amina would do it because of your orders. I could go on and on listing a thousand reasons why Philip can continue deceiving himself and ruining his life."

"But it's not just that: Amina told me that in the end, Philip, or Pip, as she calls him, will get into trouble with the law."

"But of course: Philip is completely entangled in the web and needs a large sum of money to redeem Violet from Sam, or so he believes. What do you think that package we saw exchanged between the two was?"

"I don't know. Do you?"

"I deduced it: the keys to the pawnshop where Philip works. They're going to rob it, and within a few days, even if no one provides a tip to finally frame him, the police will arrest that boy. It's a plot too easily discovered, even for Lestrade, and he'll collapse at the first interrogation, if I understand the type."

"My God! Your poor Helen will die because of this."

"Oh, well, it doesn't necessarily have to end that way, after all. Let's see... I need to send a couple of notes. Please call a messenger. And this afternoon, your house must be locked. Some important people will be put out but it will be worth it."

"Is there anything else?"

"Prepare me an outstanding disguise this time, something easy: an elegant gentleman."

6.   Game of Mirrors

At half past six in the afternoon, Violet the Red, wearing a modest dove-colored dress quite different from what she usually wore at work, stepped off an omnibus and knocked on Clara's door. An impeccable liveried butler ceremoniously opened the door and ushered her inside, escorting her wordlessly to a private sitting room on the ground floor, richly adorned with carpets, mirrors, and sofas. Sitting in an armchair, a man with glasses and a well-groomed beard watched her enter.

"Good afternoon, dear Sir. Thank you for the invitation," she said casually, after glancing at the man.

"Thank you for coming."

"Why would I refuse? You wrote to come at six and you'd have five pounds for me. Where are they?"

"Here, on the table. Thank you, there's no need for you to start undressing. I apologize for the ambiguity of the message, but what I actually need is for you to talk to me."

Violet put her stole back on, a bit surprised.

"Well, of all the things I've been asked in my experience this is perhaps the strangest."

The man calmly lit a cigarette, exhaling a bluish ring upwards.

"Actually, I mean to discuss business with you. You are well-known beyond the neighborhood: Violet the Red, one of the greatest beauties in London. My idea is to promote a new luxury establishment, in agreement with your boss, Sam, with you as the star."

"Why don't you discuss it directly with Sam?"

"I will, but first I need to make sure he won't deceive me. It only makes sense if you attract the clientele, at least in the beginning. And there are rumors that you're about to get married."

"What?!"

"To a certain Philip Barrister. You see, for me, it's an investment of hundreds of pounds."

The woman burst into laughter with a suddenly shrill voice.

"Pip! So there are two of you believing in that fairy tale, you and poor Pip! Let me tell you something: It's all nonsense. That poor fool fell in love with me. What can I say, when I told him I admired him for dedicating his life to that poor crippled sister of his, he fell for it like a fool. No, believe me, I have no intention of quitting my line of work, and starting tonight, Pip will vanish. Nine out of ten, he'll end up in jail unless he throws himself into the river because... But you haven't told me your name yet."

"You're right. My name is Jack Barrow, and I'm a friend of Philip's."

Coldness fell over the woman's face.

"That guy? I see. But then I don't understand what you want from me."

"I told you. Talk. And you did. Philip will leave you."

Violet jumped up and angrily headed towards the door.

"What a despicable charade! It's your word against mine. You're quite the cunning one, aren't you? I thought you were smarter!"

The slamming of the door echoed for a few seconds as Barrow continued to smoke in silence. Then, with a sigh, I stood up, took off the fake glasses and beard, and walked towards the main mirror.

"Yet she should be familiar with trick mirrors, poor Violet. Clara, bring him here, please."

A moment later, Clara, still dressed as a butler, entered the room, guiding Philip by the elbow. Pale as a ghost, the young man walked like a robot, his gaze lost in emptiness. I had dragged him into the adjacent sitting room half an hour earlier, telling him that I knew about his love and that I had a pleasant surprise for him. The poor lad had gone from disbelief to joy, only to witness in dismay what was happening on the other side of the glass, and to have a world of illusions and hopes come crashing down on him. He had been cruelly betrayed the very first time he dared to open up to the future. I looked at him critically as he slumped into a seat and buried his head in his hands without uttering a sound.

"I subjected you to this torture, Mr. Barrister, because you would have never believed my word. Now you realize the horrible trick that has been played on you?"

Philip seemed not to listen. He swayed slightly, muttering incomprehensible words to himself, and I could understand why. I placed a hand on his shoulder.

"Forgive me. I'm sorry for you, but you will recover."

A hysterical laugh was the response I received.

"You're joking, Mrs. Watson. I have ruined myself forever. And I have ruined my sister, which breaks my heart the most."

"No need for Helen to know about this, after all. Who wants her to hear what is only known in Whitechapel?"

"Heaven help me! I am a thief! I stole from my sister's purse! And a little while ago, thieves looted the shop where I work because, poor fool that I am, I gave them the keys in exchange for Violet's ransom! The police will trace it back to me, and I'll spend my life in prison. And I deserve it, if ever anyone did. There is no salvation for me."

"Tut-tut, such dramatic tones, my boy," I said, looking at him sternly. "Certainly, you were a colossal fool and committed a criminal act. However... you should know that, by a strange turn of events, what you gave to Mr. Sam were not the keys to his shop."

"What?!"

"Or rather, they are no longer the keys. Shortly after closing time, a blacksmith - introduced to me by a friend of mine, a 'lock-breaker' with whom he regularly collaborates - changed the lock without the owner's knowledge. And at the moment, there is a group of frustrated burglars in Whitechapel, very angry with the one who guaranteed the success of the operation. Poor

Violet will have her hands full defending herself from the knocks she'll get once they're out of jail.

"Oh, yes, jail, because I reported the matter to Scotland Yard, which has started taking me seriously lately given my associations, and they surely sent someone to catch them in the act. Besides, the girl can console herself because after last night's fiasco, sooner or later some young upstart will replace Sam with a series of knifings. That's life: easy come, easy go. And so, to come back to you, there was no crime, just a series of foolish acts that I hope you won't repeat. Go home to your sister, who can't wait for you to find a nice, sensible girl to chat with and weave lace for the grandchildren. Go, before I change my mind!"

7. From Mary's Diary

Rome, June 12, 1889
After fifteen days, I have finally embraced John again - it's incredible how long it felt without him - and I admit that not being able to tell him what truly happened to me weighs on me. Not only because of the lies I had to invent - lying to him hurts me - but also because I cannot share a part of my life with him, a part that is becoming important to me. On the other hand, I can't tell him more than what I already have after he discovered me: He could never accept that I take risks, that I put myself in danger. Perhaps in the future, when he will better understand me, I will reveal my secrets to him.

Now we have a vacation ahead of us, something I have always dreamt of, time for us in Italy to wander, observe, talk, understand each other. Love each other.

And what remains of the last adventure in the end? A saved girl, the brother of a friend pulled out of the clutches of a wicked fate. Two small drops in the sea of infamy that swirls beneath our fragile surface, a fragment of evil avoided in the face of the enormity of what still happens below us. Yet, I have done something. Whether little or much, it is still something. I will be content with that.

THE ADVENTURE OF THE LOVE-STRUCK UNIONIST

1.   An interesting book

I closed the book, captivated. I had read it almost in a hurry, savoring every page and immersing myself in each character: perhaps because I knew that those characters were more real than invented, more a product of the author's observation than his imagination. The title was "A city girl": It had been published a few months earlier, and the author, Jude Law, told the story of a girl from the East End, her hopes, her downfall. In essence, a classic tale of a poor girl seduced and abandoned by a wealthy scoundrel who had taken advantage of her, but the brilliance of the descriptions, the vivid sense of reality emanating from them, revealed a long acquaintance with those environments, a deep understanding of those dramas.

After all, I had seen and known other stories like that, especially since I frequented the poor neighborhoods: not that such affairs didn't happen everywhere, but in Whitechapel or Islington, dramas of that kind took on an even more dramatic color, as if they were the final drop in lives always poisoned by misfortune. Falling lower than where one already was in those parts meant reaching the lowest rung, being cast into the deepest circle of hell.

I had met many good people trying to help in that tragic corner of London, a corner that I discovered every day was becoming larger and expanding: those from the Salvation Army, Catholic priests with their cardinal, lay people and atheists too working out of a spirit of simple human solidarity. But the author of that book possessed a strength, a disillusioned capacity for observation, a disarming lack of rhetoric and false piety that highlighted an original and profound perspective.

I had to meet him, I reflected as soon as I closed the volume, while John smoked his pipe, with his eyes half-closed, exhausted from a day of tireless work. My young husband didn't spare himself in his work and was always available, I knew, even for those families without means and without any possibility of getting help: our finances didn't benefit from it, and perhaps neither did his health, undermined by such tireless labor, but the serenity with which he smiled at me from his armchair during those rare moments of rest showed clearly that it was the best choice for him, and for me as well.

However, getting in touch with an author in London proved to be not as easy as it seemed. I wrote to the publisher several times without receiving a response, until I finally decided to go there in person, in the vicinity of Fleet Street: a babel of reams of paper, the smell of printing, piles of books, and great confusion, amidst which I tried for a long time to speak with any employee to have the opportunity to meet Mr. Law. At that name, each person referred me to someone else, shifting from an attitude of surprised approval to one of frank embarrassment, until I insisted, clearly stating that I demanded the address - or contact information - for Mr. Law, threatening to inform my husband, who was well connected to Scotland Yard, and his friend, Inspector Lestrade. It wasn't the last time I boasted of connections I didn't actually have, and as always happened to me, the doors opened wide at the magical word "police." A furtive-eyed employee gave me an anonymous postal address, warning me to prepare for a surprise. After a series of requests from me and terse replies in return, I managed to overcome the reluctance of this peculiar author and finally arranged a meeting in a tearoom in Westminster.

2.　　From Mary's Diary

London, March 12, 1889
A surprise had been announced to me, and a surprise I indeed had. A young woman showed up at the appointed meeting, who introduced herself with a disarming smile as Margaret Harkness: She is Jude Law.

"A male pseudonym," she told me, "opens many closed doors. And that alone should make us reflect." And indeed, she was absolutely right. That marked the beginning of a fascinating afternoon and a developing friendship. I had to explain to Margaret that far from being disappointed to find a woman instead of the man I expected, I was even more pleased. We spoke at length about her experiences and mine among the underprivileged. In her book, the girl is aided by the Salvation Army, and we both know people who work there. However, she agreed with me that the rigidity of a military organization (because that's exactly how they are structured) can be helpful on the practical level but makes it very difficult to have genuine empathy for those who don't belong to that "army." And this coming from the daughter of an officer and the wife of a former soldier.

Margaret also has many connections in the Catholic world: apparently, the old Cardinal is very active in organizing and helping others, regardless of their beliefs or religious professions, assuming they have any. She also mentioned a letter sent to her by someone named Friedrich Engels, belonging to a group of intellectuals who frequent the British Museum and theorize a radical change in society, without which they argue that these social disasters will continue. It seems to be a decidedly extreme perspective, but she described it as interesting.

London, July 10, 1889

For weeks, I've been alternating between my involvement in the slums and the more or less fierce discussions with those who revolve around the British Museum. Two of these individuals are Eleanor Marx and her life partner, Edward Aveling. I confess that I've been keeping John in the dark about some of these friendships, especially the more compromising ones.

Edward and Eleanor, for example, advocate for free love and live together even though he is married, and both are active socialist militants. John is a conservative, and he certainly wouldn't share their ideas, and he would probably have difficulty accepting that I associate with them. I myself am very uncertain about it, and besides, I don't even talk about it with the Catholics who revolve around the Cardinal, who increasingly often entrust me with desperate cases and families to take care of, especially among the workers in the docks, where the Catholic Church is very active.

It's a curious situation for me, an Anglican bourgeois woman, mingling with Catholics and socialists. But everyone must do what they can wherever they find themselves, and it's not my fault that my vicar never goes to the poor people.

London, August 15, 1889

When John caught me in the Cardinal's study two months ago, while he believed I was visiting an old, non-existent aunt, and I had to confess my social activities to him, it was a painful but liberating moment for me. I felt guilty for not being able to confide in him such an important part of me, an activity that has increasingly taken up a significant portion of my life. And he is too intelligent and sensitive a man not to have understood it.

We discussed it at length during our Roman vacation, which resulted from his adventure with Holmes regarding the "little affair of the Vatican cameos," as he put it, and we realized that each of us must respect the autonomy of the world the other lives in, for the needs of our souls: his investigations with Holmes for him, my social activities for me; deep friendship with the detective for him, friendship with strange people he doesn't even know for me. The foundation of our love is respect and acceptance of each other's choices.

I haven't told him, nor will I, that sometimes my social activities lead me to seek the truth in the dramas of the people I come across, or that I occasionally disguise myself and seek the help of Holmes and the police. I need to protect him from the fear he has of losing me.

Meanwhile, here in London, the situation has exploded. One can observe the simmering of a boiling pot for a long time, one can listen to the murmuring for a long time, but it is futile to delude oneself into thinking that the lid will not eventually blow off: The strike of the workers down at the Docks has erupted. The pulsating heart of the city's trade, the vibrant underground of commerce and business, the mass of humanity that no one ever notices when strolling peacefully in the City or on Oxford Street, without which London would be an enormous fireplace without firewood. The newspapers are filled with catastrophic headlines and reports on what is happening, which, in my opinion, are entirely biased. Some are already calling for police and military intervention...

Certainly, I will not stay holed up at home waiting for the riots to gradually subside before immersing myself again in that world to find "my" families and "my" acquaintances. Surely, now more than ever, I will have to use disguises, covers: An elegant lady mingling among the ragged would be seen as a provocateur, at best. If what I read is true, emotions are running high, and we must respect the frustration of those who are agitated. As always, I will turn to Clara: I have become skilled, but her arsenal of tricks and clothes is truly impressive.

London, August, 16, 1889
After many pleas, Clara agreed to help me. I am always struck by her dual attitude towards the world of outcasts: deeply immersed in that world, she is accustomed to moving fearlessly among criminals and prostitutes, yet she is closely tied to the respectable and upper-middle-class world to which her clients belong, unsuspected members of the "good" part of society, to which she ultimately also belongs. It's as if she accepts as an inevitable fact that this society causes social disasters. And it's as if she fears the same outcasts among whom she's accustomed to moving as soon as they start talking about strikes and revolts. Or perhaps it's the Mary who associates with socialists speaking through me?

3.   In the boiling chaos

I left Clara's house a bit perplexed, dressed as a not-so-poor worker, and headed straight to the docks. The closer I got to the river, the more people I encountered: groups of people from all walks of life, every profession, every art of making a living, united only by poverty and anger. Matchgirls, in a struggle since May, dock workers, stevedores, various types of porters, and dozens of other specialized workers, along with their women and children, discussing different demands, meeting their representatives there, on the streets, in the alleys. Their leaders were there, some well-known even to me: Tom Burns, for example, with his famous light-colored hat, a thorn in the side of all the conservative newspapers, who had entered and exited the Her Majesty's prisons in recent months because of his verbal attacks.

At one point, in a small square right in front of the locked Victoria Docks, with a row of officers guarding it, I slipped into a more agitated crowd. Women in black dresses, men with crossed arms, attentively listening to the words of the speaker, a young man in his thirties, a boy it seemed: He stood at the center of the group, all impassioned. He used difficult terms, words not immediately understandable to those pure Cockneys listening to him, yet they struggled to understand, chewing on those new words.

"Bread, of course. That's what you want and ask for, fair pay for a fair hour, allowing a man to feed his family. But it must not be enough, it cannot be enough: because they must give us bread. But also roses."

"Roses? We don't need flowers."

"But yes! Time is needed to appreciate flowers, beauty, to read books, to love your wives and husbands. Because you are not beasts of burden, fit only for working, eating, and sleeping. You are men and women, and you won't give away your lives for a few shillings or barely enough bread to feed yourselves. You want fair pay but also the time to not die at work, the time you need to go out with your women or men, to admire the scenery. You are not beasts, as the masters believe! You are humans!"

And women, I thought, clutching the meager shawl Clara had given me. That boy was right, I thought, gazing at the fiery expression in his eyes and the fist raised towards the sky.

"He's right," murmured a girl next to me, with a cigarette in her mouth.

"He's right, yes!" added another. "When I'm with my Tom in the evening, we are so exhausted that we can barely stand, and not just from hunger."

"The roses, yes, damn it! The roses! We want to live, damn it!"

"But what is she doing here?"

That sentence, shouted just a few steps away from us by an old woman, seemed to clash with the chorus of agreement that was building. A girl was shoved, insulted. It was a moment and the repressed fury, the exasperation, produced their effects.

"What are you doing here? Italian, cursed scum! You came to steal our jobs! Your brother hasn't been seen among us for days, he disappeared as soon as the strike began! A scab, I bet!! Working secretly somewhere, and he sent you to see what's going on, huh?"

"Ice cream peddlers! Pimps!"

The girl couldn't react. Caught in the middle, she defended herself by covering her face, trying to deny, but the situation became increasingly dangerous, until finally a disheveled woman stood in front of her, spat at her with hatred, and moved to attack her, throwing her to the ground. I don't know what came over me: Perhaps the excitement of the moment, perhaps seeing that poor girl at risk of being beaten to a pulp, but I found myself - me, who has always been afraid of physical violence - grabbing that woman from behind and throwing her aside, standing in front of the fallen Italian girl with the posture of a hissing cat.

"Try me, sweetheart, not this flea that can't even stand!" I hissed.

The other woman, menacing, stepped forward, and for a moment we locked eyes, determined, ferocious. To this day, I wonder what had come over me and why. It was the cry of a third woman that stopped us, as the strong arms of a man intervened between us, and someone else helped the Italian girl to her feet.

"What are you doing? Rose, you stupid woman, don't know what you're saying. Her brother is at home because the police beat him to a pulp last week. They wanted him to give up the names of our leaders, but that boy didn't talk. Shame on you! And all of you, take it out on the company bosses, not the comrades! Italians and English, either we stand together or they'll crush us forever!"

The woman retreated, embarrassed, murmuring apologies, but her hate-filled gaze never left me. I turned to the young Italian, still shaken, who thanked me wholeheartedly.

"You risked your life, you know? We were both moments away from being beaten. Why did you do it, when you don't even know me?"

"I hate it when so many people gang up on one person. Is it true what they said about your brother?"

"Are you surprised? Beating up a worker is easy. If he's Italian, they beat him twice as hard. It's him, the boy who was talking earlier that they desperately wanted to know the name of. Did you see how he can stir up people? He's full of enthusiasm and knows how to reach people's hearts."

"And you know him?"

"Of course, I know him! We all know him in Saffron Hill, but I won't tell you his name. You'll have to find out for yourself if you're interested!" She concluded with a laugh, finally relaxed.

She spoke beautiful English, albeit with a strong Cockney accent, and she explained that she had arrived in London many years ago, when she was still a child. She told me her name was Paola, in Italian, but she preferred to be called Polly. She worked as a seamstress when she could, and she was very talented. She shared these details with me as I accompanied her home to recover a bit. They lived in the heart of the Italian neighborhood, around Saffron Hill, although calling that place "home" was an insult to the English vocabulary—small, dark, and oppressive as it was. Not that I was particularly surprised, considering what I had seen since I started working in the poor areas. But perhaps I had never seen so many children running in the alleys, pale and emaciated, so many women with vacant gazes begging for a bit of bread, so many young girls looking around shamefully, waiting for a man to pay them for their services.

I bid the girl farewell, promising her that I would visit her soon, and I ventured back into the neighborhood. As I looked around, contemplating the brilliant idea that Sherlock Holmes had recruited at least some of those boys as his "Irregulars," giving them some money and a bit of dignity, a role, a name that distinguished them from an anonymous and hopeless humanity, I heard someone call me in a hushed voice. It was an Irish Catholic priest whom I had worked with on the Cardinal's assignment a few weeks earlier.

"Mrs. Watson, you here! And in those clothes! I could hardly recognize you. Why?"

"I certainly can't come among these people in an evening dress. If I want to talk to them, I must be on their level. If it's not a conversation, it's charity. And I want to get to know them, understand them if I can. Please don't betray me. What about you? Isn't this an environment full of radicals and senselessness?"

The priest spread his arms, smiling.

"The Samaritans were considered heretics and enemies of the Temple even more than the socialists are today. Yet Jesus pointed to one of them as an example. The Cardinal always tells us that. And besides, the workers have their reasons, which doesn't mean I'm for socialist revolution. Although sometimes I'm tempted..."

"Yes, but it seems to me that the Catholic Church sees it a bit differently. Don't you speak about urging employers to take responsibility for the welfare of their workers? It seems to me that you don't entirely agree with the inevitability of a class struggle and that you're closer to the positions of the union rather than the socialists. After all, even the union asks for 'fairness' in wages and living conditions from the bosses. But according to Engels, capitalists can't be 'fair' by definition, and that's why, according to him, the only solution is a revolutionary one. But maybe it's too complicated for me. Taking a stance, I mean, more than making grand speeches, I simply do what I can."

"And what does doing 'what you can' entail? I've never seen you around here, but from how you speak, you seem more like an intellectual than one of us," interrupted the young man from the rally a while ago, the young unionist whose name I still didn't know, who apparently had finished addressing the crowd for the moment and was now walking away alone.

The priest took the opportunity of the interruption to bid farewell, perhaps afraid of revealing too much in the previous conversation, leaving me alone with the young man.

"If by 'one of you' you mean a unionist, then no, I'm not one. And I'm not a worker either, as my attire might suggest. But if you want to know which side I'm on, then I believe I stand on the same side as you, because I strive to fight injustices and alleviate the suffering of the poor. And I'm not an intellectual, even though I've had a good education because I consider myself more of a woman of action. And if you get to know me, you'll see that for yourself. My name is Mary. Nice to meet you."

"You certainly have a fiery character. And it's also true that you're quite a looker. It might be interesting to get better acquainted because I still haven't quite figured out if you agree with Engels or not."

"Well, it's one or the other; either Engels is right, and the capitalists inherently, by definition, have different interests from the workers, and then it doesn't make sense to ask them about being 'just,' 'good,' 'honest,' and the only way is a revolutionary one. Or if they can be 'converted,' if an appeal can be made to their good hearts, then the social doctrine of the Church is better, as it seeks to bring everyone together in the name of God and prevent conflicts. On the contrary your work needlessly inflames passions without constructiveness and without results."

"But listen to this gossip! We will achieve results, you bet! Reduction of working hours! Increase in wages! More humane working conditions and care for occupational diseases and risks of accidents! And the bosses will understand that it's in their best interest not to anger us too much, because otherwise they'll be left without profit. No profit for us, no profit for them. But listen to this, listen..."

"Do you know that the Italian boy that old woman was talking about, that was beaten to protect you? Think about what benefit he gained from having you as a representative! You talk, incite the anger of the workers, and provoke the repression of the bosses, and in the end, it's 'your' workers who suffer! And besides, you're rude! Do you know you didn't even introduce yourself?"

In short, we ended up in a pub drinking a half-and-half. Not exactly what one would expect from a good bourgeois lady, but many of the absolute certainties of my Edinburgh school days had gone down the drain, and I had discovered, along with the desire to make this world a fairer place, a longing for freedom, a craving for imagination, a fascination with novelty that had made me more confident, braver, and more unconventional.

Finally, he introduced himself as Robert Brown, apologizing for his rudeness and also for the beating the Italian worker had received because of him. He was a handsome young man with marked but regular features, black eyes and hair, an olive complexion, athletic, and taller than average. He appeared to be in his thirties, but when he spoke, he had the freshness and liveliness of a young boy. Educated and well-prepared, he knew how to skillfully defend his ideas, appealing to emotions as well. I talked to him about my social commitment, keeping silent about my interest in certain personal cases, which he showed definite attentiveness and curiosity towards. It was a stimulating and enjoyable couple of hours, and with the help of beer, we had become almost friends by the end.

Then he made a mistake. I had already noticed that in the last half hour, he was looking at me with a different gaze, staring intensely. At one point, he attempted to take my hand in his. I immediately pulled back, offended. He certainly wasn't obliged to know that I was a married woman, of course, but I didn't believe I had given him any reason for such behavior. I made my marital status clear right away and abruptly declared that I wasn't interested in any romantic involvement. Supporting progressive, even rather radical ideas was fine, but professing and practicing free love was not my cup of tea. I had already realized that when I spent time with Edward and Eleanor Aveling, whom I cared for but whose lifestyle often embarrassed me.

Once the appropriate distance had been restored, Robert suggested that before heading home, I should attend a meeting that, in his opinion, would convince me of the adequacy of their trade union policy.

The meeting was held at the union's central headquarters, a kind of huge empty warehouse located between the docks and Whitechapel. We arrived when the discussion was already well underway, and it wasn't easy for me to orient myself among the various positions expressed with extreme vigor from all sides, with exacerbated tones and overlapping shouts that made understanding the words themselves impossible.

The air was unbearable due to the smoke that had saturated the place, the gas lighting was definitely inadequate and made my eyes tear up and burn from the moment I entered. I felt dizzy and disturbed, and after just a few minutes, all I wanted was to get out, back onto the street in the fresh air. On the contrary, as soon as Robert entered, he transformed. He became excited, fervent, jumping from one side to the other, engaging with everyone, now agreeing with one person, now strongly opposing another. But it was clear that this was his environment, the place where he felt completely at ease, the atmosphere that completely captivated him, making him forget everything else. And everyone else. I had been brought there so that I could appreciate their choices, their programs, their organization, and suddenly, I became invisible, transparent, inconsequential. Somewhat disappointed, I headed towards the door I had entered from when I heard someone calling out to me:

"And what are you doing here? Didn't you say you were going back home?"

To my surprise, it was Polly, sitting on a bench, red-faced, sweaty, slightly breathless.

"And what are you doing here?" I replied. "I left you at home, barely able to stand, and here I find you, among these fanatics, with all this smoke that certainly doesn't favor your recovery."

"You're right, you're right, but Billy, my brother - we call him that even though his real name is Guglielmo - is still too battered to leave the house, and he begged me to come and hear what they're saying here. He's troubled by the things he's heard about himself, and he also has some concerns about his friend, the boy you also met. It's too important for him... and for all of us, actually."

"I see. Well, go ahead. It means that when I come to see you in the next few days, you'll report what they're saying to me as well. I can't stand it in here; I absolutely need to breathe."

I left her and, slowly making my way through the growing crowd, I accidentally bumped into a frail, dirty, trembling old man, to whom I immediately apologized.

"Oh, Mrs. Mary, it's nothing. It's always a pleasure to see you, no matter the circumstances," Sherlock Holmes whispered in response.

"And how is it that you always appear in the most unexpected places? What are you doing, following me? Are you afraid I'll get into trouble? Or no, let me guess: You're spying on these people on behalf of the government!" I continued, infuriated and disappointed. "Your brother must be involved, I bet! But you see, these are good people, maybe a bit too hot-headed, but they have their reasons! But I suppose you can't understand... Don't you dare harm them, otherwise, this time, I..."

"Mrs. Mary, Mrs. Mary, calm down!" he continued in a low but firm tone. "I'm not here to spy on anyone, at least not on those whom you care about, and certainly not on behalf of the government. I'm here for my personal investigation, the most important investigation of my life. There's a character, a criminal, a villain without scruples who is proving to be a true genius of crime. He never personally compromises himself, preferring to live in an apparently respectable way as a scientist, a high-level mathematician, but he's at the center of a large network, pulling the strings, advising, informing, manipulating, blackmailing, giving orders, and even imposing death sentences, always carried out by hired assassins.

"This monster is always ready to take advantage of moral degradation, social disorder, and the breaking of rules, and therefore, he's here too. Not personally, obviously, but hovering among this smoke, ready to exploit the first useful opportunity. His henchmen are here to stir up trouble, to insert themselves into strategic positions, to manipulate the crowds and lead them where their master desires. But I've hindered him several times this year, and I will do it again on this occasion. It has become personal now: Either him or me, there's no room for both of us in this world."

"Holmes," I whispered in a barely audible voice, so that name wouldn't resonate in such a risky environment. "You're scaring me. I've never seen you so chillingly determined. For a moment, darkness filled my heart."

"I'm sorry if I've troubled you because of me, but you're right: I'm determined like never before, and I won't stop at anything until I bring him to justice."

"All right, but please be careful. I take it that this criminal is very dangerous, and you're certainly too valuable, not only to those who care for you but also for the entire British people."

4.   From Mary's Diary

London, August 16, 1889

Yesterday was one of the most intense days of the past two years. It seemed endless. After leaving the union assembly, I went back to Clara's to change, and I returned home late in the evening, where I painfully realized that Theresa, who is proving to be not much better than Mary Jane, had done nothing about dinner. I found John quite upset, although he didn't say a word explicitly, remaining absorbed in his newspaper.

I tried to make it up to him by quickly reworking a leftover lamb roast, which, minced, sautéed in a pan with a mix of vegetables, and baked for a few minutes after covering it with mashed potatoes, also a leftover from yesterday, turned into a mouthwatering shepherd's pie.

The conversation, restored thanks to my culinary skills, inevitably turned to the riots that the whole of London is talking about, and I made sure not to inform John that I had firsthand experience of it. I simply told him that, at one of the locations of my charitable activities, I had met a young Italian seamstress named Polly who had been knocked down by the crowd and injured. She had come to get medical treatment, and after giving her some basic care, I offered to help her by accompanying her home in a hansom cab. The grateful young woman promised to mend some of my clothes for me. I didn't mention anything about union meetings, unionists, let alone brilliant and dangerous criminals.

In turn, John merely acknowledged that the working conditions of the laborers should certainly be improved but expressed a critical view of the path the demands have taken.

London, August 17, 1899

This morning, I went to visit Polly to check on her health and that of her brother Billy. I found them both better, and in fact, he seems ready to get back on his feet. However, the most worrying news doesn't concern them: it appears that Robert Brown has been arrested, and it's unclear why. What is certain is that for some obscure reason, the union lawyers do not intend to defend him. There will be another assembly in the afternoon, and presumably, we will learn more there. I cannot help but attend.

5.   A Defamatory Accusation

That same afternoon I went back to the large warehouse where the union assemblies were held, after stopping by Clara's house to change. My friend was free, so I took the opportunity to briefly update her on my discovery of a reality I knew nothing about until that moment. But Clara, with her intuition that I had already had occasion to appreciate and which made her an extraordinary woman, was able to read much more into my words than what I explicitly said.

"So, the handsome union activist caught your attention, huh?" she exclaimed.

"Is it that obvious? Or are you just particularly perceptive? Anyway, there's no point in denying it with you. I had a nice afternoon, yes, and I didn't mind being courted. But you also know that I have no intention of indulging in reprehensible behavior, and I know how to control my emotions in the moment. It's not even too difficult for me because I have a strong anchor to hold on to, which is my love for John and the certainty of his love for me. Everything I am experiencing on my own, which is deeply transforming me and giving me a sense of my worth, would mean nothing if I felt that it could jeopardize my marriage. I would be ready to stop immediately if I continued and risked losing John."

"I know, by now I think I know you well enough. But, let me tell you, you would have had all the qualities for a more - let's say - adventurous life..."

"The adventures I'm facing are enough for me, I assure you, without getting entangled in romantic affairs.

But I want to attend this assembly to understand what Robert is accused of. It's true that he has a hot temper, but his speeches didn't seem so fiery as to be considered crimes. He didn't seem like a violent inciter of crime..."

"Okay, but try to stay clear-headed and not let your sympathy for him influence you. If the union lawyers have decided not to defend him, there must be something strange going on."

"Everyone should be entitled to a fair trial and adequate defense. And I don't think he has the money to afford a lawyer."

"It seems like your intentions are already quite clear. I repeat: Be careful to see things clearly as you have always done. I won't say anything else."

The assembly was, if possible, even more crowded than the one I had attended two days before, and the atmosphere was just as choking with smoke. But this time I was determined to to last it through, at least until I understood the situation better. Before I could even recognize Polly among the crowd, standing next to her brother, and wave to her from a distance, the one who introduced himself as Attorney Penfield, one of the union's lawyers, took the floor. Penfield confirmed that Robert Brown had been arrested the previous night, but the accusation had nothing to do with his political activism. The accusation, supported by a mysterious witness, was embezzlement against the workers. Specifically, it was alleged that Robert had taken advantage of his position to siphon money from the union's common fund. The discrepancies had already been verified through the accounting books, and it even seemed that the money had been found at his home. For this reason, the union had become a plaintiff and therefore had no intention of supporting his defense. Obviously, the young man had declared himself innocent, but he had been taken to jail and put in isolation.

After this news from the lawyer a furious uproar ensued between those who felt betrayed by Robert and had already condemned him without even waiting for a trial, and those who, almost incredulous, remembered his political fervor, generosity, and availability to everyone.

I had heard enough. The accusations seemed unbelievable to me as well, but I felt deeply confused and unequipped to handle such a complicated situation. I needed help, someone with whom I could devise some defense strategy, assuming I could take on the task. Clara was the only person who seemed reliable and capable of providing me with the clarity she had urged me to have but that I felt completely lacking. I was heading towards the exit to go back to Clara when I heard someone calling me. It was Polly, who was also leaving and invited me to wait before leaving because her brother, who was following her slowly, leaning on a crutch, wanted to talk to me about something important. So, I stopped and waited for him in front of the warehouse, after finding a corner where we could speak in peace.

"You were brave to defend my sister. Thank you," he began.

"It was even braver of you not to mention Robert's name despite the beatings," I replied.

"So, that's what they told you. But it's not true, not at all. They wanted something else."

"And you didn't tell the others?"

"They wouldn't believe an Italian, not even our bosses would believe us."

I couldn't let that opportunity slip away. I took him aside and started talking to him, trying to convince him, using the tones and arguments I had assimilated in those days: trust, unity, the need to fight together. It took a lot to make him feel comfortable, but in the end, he opened up.

It turned out that they beat him not because he refused to name the union bosses, who were actually known to everyone, but because they wanted him to testify against Robert, inventing baseless accusations, and he had refused. And those who beat him were not police officers but low-level criminals, the henchmen executing orders for someone who didn't want to get his hands dirty. He recognized one of them by his voice, by a pronunciation defect that he hadn't bothered to conceal like he did with his face, covered by a scarf. And he was one of Sam's men, he was sure of it. That same Sam who had already crossed my path.

"I really think there's nothing else to do," Clara said after I informed her about the situation. "We need to recruit from another source."

"What do you mean?" I asked.

"We need to find out who ordered the beating, because it's the same gang. They are surely the ones who orchestrated the accusation against your union activist..."

"He's not 'mine,' I've already told you!"

"Okay, it's just a figure of speech... What I mean is that the only source of information we have is Sam..."

"And he certainly won't come and tell us who paid him, not even if you show up with your 'lawyer'..."

"No, exactly. That's why we need help. We need to make him reveal it without realizing it."

"And when does a man let his secrets slip? I've got it! you want to use one of your friends!"

"Exactly! You got it. And I even know who. Her name is Jenny. She's beautiful, knows how to be vulgar enough to be irresistible to someone like Sam, she's cunning and very intelligent, and above all, she's trustworthy because she owes me a debt of gratitude. One day I'll tell you the details."

"I'll be happy to meet her. As they say, your friends are my friends, right? We're putting together quite an adventurous gang," I said, smiling.

"Yes, the Adventuresses of Regent Street..." Clara concluded with a hearty laugh.

The next day, I met Jenny. She was truly beautiful: Her raven-black hair framed a perfect oval face, in which her dark eyes shone brightly. Her small, slightly upturned nose gave her a playful look, while her full lips were extremely sensual. Petite and well-proportioned, she had a warm and captivating voice. She could express herself correctly, and although I personally didn't have a chance to experience the vulgarity Clara had mentioned, I had no reason to doubt that she could use it to attract that gentleman, Sam.

I immediately realized she was a clever woman because it took her no more than five minutes to understand perfectly what needed to be done and how to do it. I also liked the enthusiasm with which she was ready to get involved when she realized it was a good cause, defending an innocent person from a defamatory accusation. Of course, she wouldn't present herself under her real identity to avoid arousing suspicion in Sam, but she would pretend to be a common girl, perhaps a worker or a saleswoman, approaching him as if she happened to be in his establishment.

So, we dressed her in more modest attire than what she usually wore, but still allowing her beauty to shine through. Clara skillfully did her makeup, enhancing her beauty without making it look unnatural, and gave her instructions on how to exude seductiveness at the proper moment, within the folds of false naïveté.

The result was undeniably explosive. Jenny went to Sam's establishment that same evening, asking for directions at the counter to reach an address nearby where she was supposed to meet a friend. Sam immediately noticed her, interrupted the conversation, and offered to accompany her personally. Jenny accepted the "stranger's" offer after some simulated resistance, and along the way, she was convinced to forget about the non-existent friend and accompany him to one of his haunts. It took the entire night, but according to Jenny, Sam let slip not only what interested us, but also boasted about dozens of other crimes he had committed. The next morning, when Jenny reported to Clara's house, we knew everything we needed to know.

Assuming that the accounting books had been falsified, we realized that we needed to verify it ourselves. I had studied some basic rudiments of economics in Edinburgh, so I felt capable and eager to investigate in that direction. However, we had to find a way to do it without raising suspicions among the culprits. With the help of a printer friend of Billy's, we fabricated a fake court order stating that I was a court clerk authorized to copy the pages of the incriminated accounting books.

Thus, with tremulous audacity, disguised as a man, I presented myself at the union headquarters, where I was seated and introduced to the accountant hired by the union to straighten out the accounts. I explained that the originals would be brought to court, of course, but the prosecutor needed copies to prepare his indictment.

I began flipping through the books while the accountant, in an instructive manner, pointed out the incriminating points, the ones indicating unjustified shortfalls and suggesting that the figures had been misappropriated by the accused. As I pretended to diligently copy, I immediately realized that those very points were written in a different handwriting that imitated the previous one but contained some unmistakably original traits. Holmes's knowledge of handwriting, allowing him to attribute a writing to a man or a woman, assess the emotional state of the writer, and identify the authorship from small details, had always fascinated me, and I had done some research on the topic. It didn't require an expert graphologist to realize that those books had been crudely falsified. At that point, I deliberately let my perplexity show on my face, causing the accountant to become alarmed.

"Why that expression? Is there something that doesn't convince you?" he asked.

"More than something. If you truly are an accountant, you cannot have failed to notice that these accounting books are falsified. And quite clumsily, I might add. Unless you were the one behind the forgery!"

"You damned spy! You'll pay for this!" he exclaimed, emerging menacingly from behind his desk.

"A real tough guy, no doubt. And now what's the matter? Just because I now have a Derringer in my hand? You are so disappointing! Anyway, it's too late now! Come out, boys! He fell for it!"

Like lightning, Billy's two friends who had accompanied me and whom I had hidden behind the door of the accountant's room rushed out of their hiding spot. We had learned from Sam that he was the one who had ordered the attack, as he had ambitions for a career in the union and feared the competition from Robert, who had quickly become popular and well-liked by both the leaders and the base. Under the threat of the two sturdy gentlemen I had brought with me, the accountant confessed everything:

"It's in your best interest to talk, they aren't policemen, just like I'm not a court officer."

"Let me go immediately. You're committing a crime."

"You're absolutely right. And it might not be the last one. You see, these boys can be a bit impulsive, and the river is nearby. You know, they might want to see how long you can float with a millstone around your neck."

"You wouldn't dare..."

"Oh, no, in fact, millstones are too heavy to move. But there are other ways. What do you think, boys? This one won't talk."

"No! Stop!" the terrified scoundrel shouted as he saw the expression on the workers' faces. "Okay. I paid Sam's gang to do the job. They brought some money to Robert's house."

"We already know that. Why did you have that Italian man brutally beaten? What did you need him for?"

"To keep from showing my hand. But the idiot didn't want to accuse him, so I had to falsify the records and accuse him myself."

"And you did a pretty lousy job, I must say. Well, all of you have heard it. You can tell everything to the union and call Scotland Yard."

"But... can't we handle it ourselves?!"

"And who's going to get Robert out of jail?"

"Uhmm... all right then. But we can still get a little satisfaction before we go. Do you mind stepping outside, Mi'lady?"

I prefer to draw a veil over what followed. Suffice it to say that the wretched accountant was escorted to prison, the charges against Robert were dropped, and his friends organized a grand celebration in his honor.

6.   From Mary's Diary

London, August 24, 1889
I saw Robert again this morning. I hadn't seen him since the day before his arrest. I didn't think it was appropriate for me to attend the celebration held for him since my cover had been

blown with the arrival of Scotland Yard, and everyone had discovered my true identity. I would have felt completely out of place. However, he insisted so much on seeing me, after sending me flowers and notes to express his gratitude. And deep down, I didn't mind seeing him either. This time, no pub: I chose the tea room of a newly opened hotel on the Strand called the Savoy. The decorated salon where tea is served has a glass dome through which natural light filters. In the center, there is a gazebo from which a pianist plays softly, without hindering conversation.

When I arrived, punctually, Robert was already there, slightly uncomfortable. He had tried to dress appropriately for the environment, moving with great caution, but one could sense his embarrassment. I was a bit cruel, perhaps, but my choice was not random: I needed to communicate to him unambiguously my belonging to another world. I didn't dress in an excessively sophisticated manner, but I was definitely elegant, albeit understated. I had no doubt that I had made an impression: He stood up to greet me but didn't know whether to shake my hand or not, while he couldn't take his eyes off me and even had difficulty uttering a few words of greeting.

I broke the ice and directed the conversation towards recounting the events. In reporting the facts, I omitted something, particularly Jenny's role in obtaining the decisive information, preferring to highlight the deductive aspects of my reasoning. When he recovered from the emotion and started talking, Robert returned to being as talkative as I knew him, expressing his gratitude not only for helping him in the matter but also because I had immediately sided with him despite appearances. I knew that this was the most delicate point, the one that revealed the most about me, as it explicitly showed feelings of friendship for him, but I was prepared to reply, and by reversing the sequence of events, I made Billy's confidence in me decisive in my decision to help him, as if that had convinced me of his innocence.

We talked a little more about the claims, the union, his new position within it, but they were words that only served to better fit into our respective roles. After the euphoria of the initial impact, we were communicating to each other that we both understood better what the true dimension of our friendship could be. A friendship that, although based on undeniable spiritual affinity, we wouldn't actively cultivate any further, knowing that if necessary, but only if necessary, each could always count on the other's help. We parted with a smile, looking into each other's eyes, knowing that no further words were needed.

I returned home with a still turbulent mind but a peaceful heart because I had clarified my feelings and intentions, and I feel that he was able to do the same. I can't wait to see John tonight. Maybe I should suggest taking a trip together.

7.   An Urgent Decision

I immediately recorded my thoughts in my diary, hastily, without even changing, and when John came home shortly after, he confirmed what an extraordinary man he is:

"Lately, your volunteer work has taken you up quite a bit," he said after embracing me, "but I can tell from your attire that you've returned to frequenting more refined environments. It has been a rather depressing time for me. You dealing with the problems of those you assist, Holmes not contacting us for days, busy as he is on a mysterious hunt for some elusive criminal. I have been very lonely, and I realized that without the two of you, I would be completely lost. I think you did well to distance yourself a bit from those degraded situations that sometimes involve you too much. I would be happy if it were something more than just a momentary choice. Would that be all right for you?"

There was no need for him to say more. A sensitive and loving man like him couldn't help but notice how differently I had been acting. Once again, he had understood me, and once again, he had found the right words to ease my way out.

"You're right, dear," I replied. "I think I will take a break for a while. I need rest. Also, I haven't told you yet, but for a few days now, I have been feeling particularly tired, exhausted, sometimes breathless, even without exerting any special effort. Perhaps it wouldn't be a bad idea for my doctor to take a look at me."

"Of course, gladly," John replied. "I couldn't ask for anything better than being able to calmly see my wife without her running off for some urgent commitment."

We laughed together, joking about it. It was the last time we did so with that carefree spirit.

THE ADVENTURE OF THE MYSTERIOUS FIANCÉ

1.　A Matter of the Heart

The month of September of 1890 was an unusually rainy month. Summer had abruptly ended, and relentless storms kept John and I mostly confined indoors. The pleasant walks in the park were now over, and only the company of a good book by the fireplace could brighten our days. However, that afternoon my husband's presence began to feel a bit cumbersome to me because I was expecting a visit from someone in need of help. I hadn't told him anything, hoping to schedule the visitor during the time John usually dedicated to his daily walk. The inclement weather, though, posed an obstacle to this meeting. In fact, it was just a few minutes before four o'clock, the appointed time for my acquaintance's visit, and he was firmly planted in his armchair with no intention of abandoning his reading of his beloved William Clark Russell. I was compelled to address the matter without fully revealing myself, as I had decided to keep the secret from him regarding the true nature of my activities.

"You know, dear, my dressmaker will be coming to see me in a few minutes. She requested a meeting to seek advice on a matter of the heart. You understand, it's women's affairs, and it would be very embarrassing for her to discuss it in front of you. On the other hand, with this rain, I wouldn't know where to take her. Could you please remove yourself for an hour?"

"My dear, you seem to be a magnet for troubles! This house is too often frequented by people in need of help. I greatly appreciate your willingness to shoulder the difficulties of the people you encounter, but it seems that all the wretched and unfortunate souls of London are drawn to you like flies to honey. It feels like I've just changed partners, it's the same things that used to happen with Holmes!" he said, disheartened.

"There's no need for you to leave; it will suffice if you leave me here in the parlor alone and go read in the bedroom. Without eavesdropping, of course!"

"Believe me, I couldn't care less about listening to your conversations. I'll gladly keep my distance. I'm just sorry I won't enjoy your company and the comfort of my armchair..."

"I promise I'll be quick, and to console you, I'll prepare your favorite fish pie for dinner tonight."

"Thank you, but I don't need to be won over by my stomach," he replied, pretending to be proud. "I'll appreciate the fish pie, although I repeat that my primary interest is being able to spend time with you. Especially since if I indulge too much in culinary pleasures, Holmes won't fail to point it out with his witty remarks as soon as he sees me. It's as if he has scales for eyes, given how precise he is in his observations regarding my weight..."

Later on, the girl arrived, and John retreated to the bedroom. The inclement weather hadn't spared her, even though she had come in a hansom cab. I hung her wet overcoat and hat on the coat rack by the entrance and invited her to sit in one of the two armchairs in front of the fireplace, allowing her boots to dry a little. Her name was Annie Spencer, and she wasn't exactly my dressmaker but a seamstress gaining experience under her. Very precise and attentive to details, she had often been assigned by the shop owner to assist me with alterations and repairs. I had come to appreciate her professionalism, as well as her modesty and courtesy, and I had taken a liking to her, a sentiment that evidently was mutual since she had asked me if and when she could talk to me about a personal matter that was very important to her and concerned a man she was seeing.

"So, Annie," I began, "you hinted at something concerning your fiancé, but you've been quite mysterious. Would you like to explain the whole matter to me from the beginning?"

"Yes, of course. I met George six months ago at a dance hall I used to frequent with a friend of mine. It's a place where young people go looking for friendships, but the management upholds certain standards, and the men who go there know they have to behave well, with respect, you know. Well, George presented himself quite nicely, bless him, and he had a handsome appearance. Moreover, he spoke well, and he was well-dressed, neat, you know. And the thing I liked most about him was that he made me laugh, really, to the point of tears, but without being vulgar. Well, not too much, anyway. You know how it is, right?"

"Not exactly, but I think I understand. Please continue."

"Anyway, we started seeing each other, and I became increasingly sure that he was a decent fellow. I liked how he treated me, always kind and understanding, and he also always gave me nice gifts. Nothing extraordinary, mind you, but flowers, chocolates, things like that. Then, a month ago, he gave me a silver chain necklace with a pendant and declared his love for me. He said he cares about me, that he really likes me, that he wants to marry me—basically, all those things a girl wants to hear."

"Good. That sounds very good. So, what's the problem then?"

"Well, you see, I don't understand why every time I try to talk about his family, his home, his neighborhood, he changes the subject. He says 'I'll tell you later,' 'it's not the right time now,' and then talks about something else. I don't understand, but it seems clear to me that there's something he doesn't want to tell me, and I'm afraid it's something bad and that he's playing with me. Am I wrong? I mean, don't you think I should know more about his background, his job, his family?"

"Of course, you're right. It's only natural that a good girl like you would want to know more about the past of a man who's even asking you to marry him, that goes without saying. You didn't tell me how old he is and what kind of job he said he does."

"Well, he didn't give me his exact age either. He says he's old enough to take care of my well-being, that I should trust him, that I shouldn't be afraid, and that his intentions are good. I would say he's four or five years older than me. I don't think he's in his thirties. As for his job, he is a dockworker at the port, even at night. I think he has always done manual labor, considering his strong and calloused hands, and his chest, may God preserve it!

He's very muscular, robust, but lean, like someone who's always on the move. He drinks beer, but not too much, and he smokes, perhaps a bit too much. I don't think he gambles because he has never shown interest in gambling establishments. I've never seen him with newspapers of that kind, nor has he ever talked to me about it."

"He seems like an ordinary young man, from how you describe him, and the fact that he hasn't told you about his past doesn't necessarily mean there's a mystery. He could be from humble origins and be ashamed of it, I don't know."

"But he knows that I'm a simple girl, from the working class. Imagine if I cared about - as you said? - origins. No, I think there's something he doesn't want to tell me."

"All right, let's start with that. We'll try to find out if you're right. What do we want to do? In order for me to form an opinion, I should meet him in person, see him, talk to him. How can we do that? Where do you usually meet?"

"The place we most often go to is a dance hall, as I told you, but we also go to parks, where he always treats me to a refreshing drink or an ice cream. But I don't know if I can manage it, a lady like you, in the places we go."

"If that's the case, don't worry, I won't let you make a fool of yourself, and I'll surprise you. It will be enough for you to introduce me as an older colleague, unfortunate, who has been abandoned by her husband and who, after a period of seclusion, needs company to overcome her melancholy. I'll take care of the rest."

"Well, if you say so... I don't know how you'll manage..."

"Trust me. I'm good at this. I'll take advantage of an afternoon when John is seeing his patients to accompany you on one of your outings to the park. To avoid arousing suspicion with your boyfriend, start talking to him about this unfortunate friend and try to understand if he would be willing to 'waste' your time together with me."

Annie left, not entirely reassured by my plan, but I remained determined. I would visit the shop in a few days to finalize the date for the appointment. I then went to free John from his seclusion and hurried to the kitchen to fulfill my culinary commitment to him, ignoring his sarcastic remarks about women's secrets.

2.   From Mary's Diary

London, September 12, 1890

Today John made me laugh when he compared the visit of my "client" to those that filled his days with Sherlock Holmes. "You have no idea how accurate you are!" I thought to myself. It's true, Holmes is one of my role models, at least in the systematic use of observation and indignation towards injustice, but I have no intention of competing with him. I don't desire it in carrying out this activity, which I have come to understand is the way I can fulfill myself while also perhaps filling some inner need. But above all, I don't desire it because I don't intend to assert any supremacy over my husband. My right to be the center of John's attention is certainly legitimate, both on a strictly legal level and on a moral level, as he has personally committed to me in that regard. But neither of these reasons are valid for me to undermine or oppose the friendship between him and Sherlock Holmes. Firstly, because their relationship predates ours, and without it, we wouldn't have even met. But most importantly, because I couldn't bear to feel responsible for the disappearance of that special light that shines in his eyes when his friend calls him to share a new adventure. That's why I have never been an obstacle to their friendship in the past, and I never will be. On the contrary, as I have always done, I will always encourage him to break away from his professional routine to occasionally experience those emotions that fighting injustice can provide. After all, isn't it the same for me?

London, September 17, 1890
Finally, yesterday I met George, Annie's boyfriend. My disguise was perfect: I didn't have to change my appearance too much. I only darkened the color of my skin slightly with powder, tousled my hair a bit, wore a slightly outdated and rather worn-out jacket over a simple and unpretentious dress. Common shoes, used but not ruined. I made sure to hide my hands, too well-kept for a seamstress, with a pair of thread gloves, clearly used but not worn out. But the masterpiece, for which Annie herself gave me great compliments later, was in the use of my voice. I made it hoarse, as Clara taught me, but above all, I modified my language, speaking more simply and using slang expressions, and imitating the pronunciation of the Londoners, whom I now know very well.

The result was brilliant, and George didn't show the slightest suspicion. He was genuinely kind and sympathetic towards my difficult personal situation. He was patient as he listened calmly even giving cautious and reasonable advice. In short, after spending an afternoon with him, I would have described him as a decent young man and therefore dismissed Annie's fears as unfounded fantasies.

However, towards the end of the afternoon, as we were walking and it was still hot, George took off his jacket and rolled up his shirt sleeves after unbuttoning the cuffs. It was a natural gesture, of someone who felt comfortable and allowed themselves to be at ease. But that gesture betrayed an excess of confidence, underestimating the power of observation of the timid and modest seamstress standing before him. On his right forearm, with traces of a very approximate attempt at erasure, a tattoo was clearly visible, consisting of initials and a date. And neither of the two letters was a 'G.' Certainly, they could have been the initials of an old flame, but why go through so much trouble to erase it? This detail, combined with his reluctance to talk about the past, directed me towards a specific hypothesis: The initials of HIS REAL name were different, and his attempt to erase them was the corollary of his identity change. But what necessitated this deception? What secret does George carry that he cannot reveal even to the woman he claims to love? What is in that past that cannot even be mentioned?

All that remains is to ask him directly, after revealing my identity and my discovery about his tattoo, assuming that my hypothesis is true.

3.   The truth doesn't always hurt

A few days after my encounter with George, I went to talk to Annie. Without revealing my suspicions, I asked her to arrange another meeting. Telling her what I thought would only alarm her, and ultimately, who was I to stir up a storm between them, perhaps without reason? After all, it was true that she had asked me to intervene because the situation was troubling her, and a woman's feelings should always be considered as evidence. It was better to be cautious and tread carefully. I also suggested that she find an excuse to step away for a few minutes after we met, leaving me alone with her boyfriend. She seemed troubled for a moment, but I reassured her:

"It will only be for a few minutes. I just need to verify something, and your presence might be an obstacle. I promise I'll explain everything to you afterward."

"I have a lot of trust in you, you know, and even though the mystery still scares me, I believe I'm right to trust you," she replied.

So, after a couple of days, I once again assumed the role of the third wheel (or rather, the third unwelcome guest) and accompanied them on another stroll in the park. We sat on the benches of an outdoor café, and as planned, Annie seized the opportunity to step away:

"I need to powder my nose, but don't order without me! I'll be quick, I promise," she said with a smile."And don't you two run off without me, I'll find you even if you're at the end of the world, huh!" she added, laughing openly to conceal the tension.

George appeared embarrassed and tried to engage in small talk about the weather, but I didn't have time to waste.

"Listen, young man, now I can't give you too many explanations," I began, with my real voice, causing him to

128

jump in his chair. "So let's get straight to the point: I know that you've changed your identity for quite some time, trying to make the world forget who you were before. Honestly, I don't care why or who you really are. I only know that I truly care for Annie, and if you ever hurt this girl, you won't just have to deal with me, but also with two of my friends who have a lot of influence at Scotland Yard. So, spill the beans quickly before Annie returns and give me a good reason not to tell her everything I know."

The boy remained stunned in silence for a moment, looking at me as if he were seeing me for the first time and contemplating whether to trust me. Then, in the calm tone I already knew from him, he replied:

"Anything to not lose the woman I love, the only one who made me feel alive again after four years when time stood still. It's true that I didn't answer Annie's questions, but I didn't tell her any lies. I'm a decent person, at least in that regard. I didn't tell her what she wanted to know because I feared that if she knew my story, she would leave me.

"I'll tell you right away why I've hidden my past: I've been in prison for a theft I committed out of desperation. It's not an excuse, I know, but the punishment was severe because I couldn't afford a lawyer, and I served it all. I behaved well in prison because I believed it when they told me that if I behaved well, I could start over once I got out. But that wasn't the case. For two years, I tried to find a job, putting in all my effort, accepting night shifts for twelve or fourteen hours a day, without holidays or breaks. However, as soon as they found out I had been in prison, they always found an excuse to let me go. They would say, 'You're good,' 'You're a hard worker, but the job market is tough, there are others with families. Come back in a while, maybe things will change.' But things never changed. So, at some point, I invented a new name, using my mother's cousin's name from Bristol, because I said I came from there, and I can do the accent a bit. And maybe if they did any checks, they would find out that there really is a George Faulkner in Bristol with a clean record.

"Everything was going well; I worked, earned money, even managed to save some, and I had fun with a few girls. Then, one day, I met Annie, and everything changed. I wanted to truly be someone else because she doesn't deserve an ex-convict like me. She's too righteous, beautiful, and honest. A thousand times I thought about talking to her and telling her everything, answering her questions, but a thousand times I couldn't find the courage to risk losing her forever.

"So, now you know everything; there isn't much more to know except that I've been a coward, but out of love. Do what you think is right."

I looked at the poor lad: his trembling hands, forced smile, and determined appearance of someone who has decided to face reality with all the courage he has, knowing that he may face defeat.

"Dear George, - can I call you George, right? - in the end, I'm glad I wasn't completely wrong about you when I initially took you for a good lad. Because deep down, you are a good lad. I won't say anything to Annie. I won't tell her anything because you will. Immediately, as soon as she returns, without further delay. I will step aside, and you will tell her the whole story. If she loves you, she will understand, especially since you have fully served your sentence, and no one has the right to make you pay anymore beyond what the law deemed right. And if she doesn't understand, then it means she doesn't love you enough to accept you as you are. And in that case, it's better for it to happen now rather than in a few years. Remember, an ugly truth is always better than a beautiful lie."

George let out a long sigh, briefly bowed his head. When he raised it again, there was a painful decision in his eyes, one that must have cost him a lot.

"All right. I'll do it as soon as she returns. Ultimately, I have to thank her for cornering me. It was really time for me to break free from this ambiguity."

"You don't need to tell me anything. I've heard it all," Annie said gravely, emerging from the hedge behind us, where she had been hiding unbeknownst to both of us. "I wonder, George – or whatever the hell your name is – if I completely misjudged your sensitivity, your ability to judge people. I wonder if you're really the sharp and thoughtful guy I thought you were. But who do you think you've met, huh? I certainly don't think I'm perfect, but I have a bigger heart than you can imagine. I truly love you, George, and if my feelings are returned with sincerity and the same passion I have, there's nothing else that can stop me. If you had trusted me earlier, you would have saved yourself months of fear and worry, and it would have been the same for me. I have to thank Mrs. Mary, and you should do the same because by clearing the sky of the clouds you created, she has set us free and allowed us to love each other freely."

4.   From Mary's Diary

London, September 23, 1890

I'm really happy to have helped Annie and George. They are two good young people who deserve to be happy. The three of us had tears in our eyes when I left them tonight, embraced on that park bench, to return to my John, my love, wondering if, perhaps, I too prefer a beautiful lie to an ugly truth. But then I reflected that, in the end, both my lives are beautiful, and it's only right to let them both continue. I can't wait to tell Holmes how I solved the case by observing the erased tattoo. It seems like a fitting application of his method of observing seemingly insignificant details.

London, March 15, 1891

This morning, I went to visit Sherlock Holmes to tell him about my latest adventures. He was at home, contemplating a case that currently captivates his attention. At least, that's what he told me. On the stairs, I caught a glimpse of a young man going upstairs to the room that used to be John's when he lived there and still occasionally uses when Holmes needs his help with a case. I didn't need to ask Holmes about it because he read the curiosity in my eyes. He told me the young man is a temporary guest at 221B Baker Street and, in this regard, he asked me to have dinner with us tomorrow evening because he wants to discuss this matter with the two of us without the guest. "With the two of you," he said exactly that. Holmes has been a bit strange lately, indeed.

Speaking of Annie and George, Holmes showered me with compliments for the observation about the tattoo because he said it reminded him of a story from his youth that was pivotal in his career choice. It's a story, he told me, that he had just shared with John but hasn't been published yet. It's yet another time I've surprised him by demonstrating that I reason like him, and according to him, it hasn't been a common experience with the women he has known—only one other woman in the past gave him the same feeling.

5.   The Five Orange Pips

The evening we spent with Holmes at our home was unforgettable. There was a strange, solemn atmosphere, as if it were a grand occasion. Perhaps it was a bit too much for an evening among old friends, such as John and I considered ourselves to be, but it was the first time he had visited us, and I wanted to make a good impression. For the occasion, I sought advice from Mrs. Hudson because I didn't trust my culinary skills. The result was that we had the best of Scottish tradition for dinner. We started with a potato and haddock soup, with a spicy and intense aroma but delicate flavor, which I decided to pair with a fine Montrachet, Holmes's favorite, as a tribute to him. The main course was haggis with mashed potatoes and turnips, accompanied by a whisky sauce, served together with Yorkshire pudding and accompanied by a vintage Bordeaux, one of our friend's favorites. We finished with cranachan, the typical Scottish raspberry dessert. Without false modesty, I must say it was an extraordinary success.

The conversation during dinner did not address the matter on which Holmes wanted to hear our opinion. It was, as often happened with him, extremely varied and interesting. We ranged from beekeeping to medieval music, from muzzle-loading firearms to bicycle tires, without any interruption or limits to the enjoyment.

After dinner, once they had showered me with compliments and I had dodged them properly, the two men opened a bottle of Port, kept for a special occasion, and lit two robust cigars. I settled into my rocking chair next to the open window, the only way to survive in that artificial fog, even though it was decidedly cold outside. To endure, I covered myself with a shawl. I began rocking back and forth, smiling at the thought that John had given me that rocking chair, envisioning the moments when we would rock our little ones.

"Mr. Thomson, my temporary guest," Holmes began, "has received a substantial death threat, as a result of which he is in constant and real danger. He lives in Sussex, on a property he has inherited, and his pursuers know it well, having already committed two murders there. He cannot return without adequate protection. However, the police did not take his fears seriously and did not see fit to protect him. That's why I invited him to stay here for as long as necessary to have those scoundrels arrested. As long as he remains in London, at my house, he will be safe because I am almost certain he wasn't followed and therefore none of them knows his current whereabouts. The problem, for which I need to consult with you, is that even if I manage to have the actual perpetrators of this murder plot arrested, the masterminds, who are far away from here, may send another assassin to kill him, and Mr. Thomson could never sleep peacefully again for the rest of his life."

"Do I need to take notes?" John asked.

"If you think it might be helpful, why not?" Holmes replied. "Thomson's uncle went to America as a young man and made a fortune with cotton plantations. He then fought with Jackson and Hood in the Confederate ranks, rising to the rank of colonel. At the end of the war, being a staunch supporter of slavery, he refused to stay in the United States and returned to Britain, where he bought the estate in Sussex. A few years ago, he received an envelope containing five orange pips, and according to his nephew, who was present when he opened it, he became extremely agitated. He immediately summoned his lawyer, Fordham, and handed him a bundle of documents from a brass chest on which the letter 'K' was engraved three times, instructing him to deliver them to the police if he died a violent death. Another part of the papers was burned by him in the fireplace. Seven weeks later, the poor man, who had lived in fear during that time, was found dead, drowned in a small pond near his residence. The subsequent investigation concluded it was suicide.

"His brother, Robert Thomson, inherited the estate. He was an inventor, quite versatile and brilliant. Among other things, he invented the non-pneumatic bicycle tires, but despite having patented them in 1847, at the age of 25, the invention was later attributed to Dunlop. A couple of years ago, Dunlop himself acknowledged Thomson's primacy, but Thomson couldn't benefit from it as he had already died. Yes, died, because he, too, received a death threat from a group calling itself the KKK a year later, along with an accompanying order this time: 'Put the papers on the sundial.' But as I mentioned earlier, the papers were partly destroyed and partly delivered to the authorities. He tried to escape, but a few days later, he was found dead at the bottom of a well. Once again, the investigation quickly closed, ruling it as an accident, but it was obviously an assassination by the KKK's henchmen."

"Holmes, what is the KKK?" John asked.

It was me who answered from my armchair:

"It's a secret American society that is racist and violent, advocating white supremacy, targeting black people and those who support them. They are murderers who should be eradicated from the face of the earth. I thought they had been dismantled."

"Mostly, yes, Mrs. Watson," replied Holmes, giving me a pleased look. "I believe it was largely thanks to the documents handed over to the authorities by the lawyers. However, my client knew that sooner or later, it would be his turn. When he received the pips, he sought help from a friend, Major Pendergast, who sent him to me. And I haven't let him leave my house for two weeks while I conducted my investigations.

"And what have you discovered?" John asked again.

"Some elements are based on my deductions, while others come from verifying my interpretations of the clues. The ritual of sending orange pips or melon seeds as an intimidating message is indeed a practice of the Ku Klux Klan, the fraternity of assassins referred to by Mary, which evidently continues to exist clandestinely. But why would the members of this terrorist organization target their own affiliate who left the United States to hold onto his segregationist beliefs? And how did he acquire the valuable property in Sussex and possess over fourteen thousand pounds in cash at his death? In South Carolina, he was the owner of cotton plantations, that's true, but with the end of slavery, the value of his possessions must have plummeted immensely. Furthermore, the choices made by the new federal government in terms of economic policy favored the interests of industry and speculators engaged in post-war reconstruction, rather than those of the plantation owners. He had little choice but to sell as best he could and leave. I should also add that during a heated conversation when he feared being killed at any moment, he referred to his inheritance as 'such a two-edged thing.' Why would he say that? What was he leaving behind, besides wealth?

"Inside the brass box where the documents were kept, Mr. Thomson remembered seeing a label that said something like 'Letters, reminders, receipts, and a register.' So, in addition to documents concerning people's identities, his uncle also dealt with receipts and records. What if he had been the treasurer of the association? That would provide a much more plausible explanation for his escape from the USA, based on that entity which annihilates all ideologies: money. The colonel escaped with the KKK's treasury, that's why they continued to search for him years after his disappearance—for revenge and to regain possession of the money. And that's why they kept asking the heirs for the documents: The source of his wealth would have been evident from the documents, as well as the 'legitimacy,' so to speak, of a compensation claim.

"As for the assassins, my investigations started with the postal stamps on the three letters sent to the two victims and Mr. Thomson: Pondicherry in India, Dundee, and East London. Three seaports, so the sender must have been on a ship. Considering the time interval between the letter's arrival and the implementation of the threat, I deduced that the letter, traveling by steamship, always arrived before the assassins because they were aboard a sailing ship. In recent days, I immersed myself in research on Lloyd's registers and other archives, following the routes of sailing ships that had departed from Pondicherry six or seven months before the first letter. I identified the relevant ship, the Lone Star, which, incidentally, is an American vessel. I also discovered that the crew consisted of Finnish and German sailors, with only the captain and the two officers being Americans. I immediately telegraphed their names to the police at the destination port, along with a detailed report of the facts to be delivered to the magistrate. With the swift methods of American justice, there would have been little left for them to do."

"Why do you say 'there would have been little left for them to do'? What else happened?" John asked, not missing a single word of the story.

"Because I learned this morning that the ship will never reach America as it was wrecked off the Isle of Wight. However, whether they're dead or in prison, the problem remains, as I told you at the beginning: Someone else will eventually seek Fred Thomson to complete the mission," Holmes concluded, disheartened.

The four of us remained silent for a few minutes. Then I had an epiphany.

"Perhaps we've had a stroke of luck."

"What do you mean?" John asked, and I saw a spark ignite in Holmes' eyes as they met mine.

"I thought of something inspired by an incident that happened to me. It's a women's story—nothing important, John. The question is: When do you stop trying to kill someone?"

"When he's already dead!" Holmes replied promptly. "And only the four of us know how things went!"

"So we let Fred Thomson die and give birth to a non-existent John Smith!" I pressed.

"But what are you saying?" John added.

"Indeed, Watson, it will be up to you to stage the murder. You're so good at inventing stories!" exclaimed Holmes.

"Wait a moment! Let me catch up with the two of you!" John exclaimed.

"It's simple," I replied, a little impatiently. "If the KKK believes that Thomson was killed by the assassins before they left, they will think there's nothing more to be done. Thank God, the assassins drowned and cannot inform them that it's not true."

"And what does it have to do with me?"

"So, - I began with a didactic tone - you will have to write a credible story in which you will say that Holmes underestimated the threats of the KKK and sent Mr. Thomson home, where he found his assassins waiting for him."

"You must assert that in such words as will carry conviction with them," Holmes added.

"But, Holmes, that would make you look bad in front of my readers! And besides, it won't be believable that you made such a mistake!"

"On the contrary, it will be even more plausible because no one will suspect that you would lie to portray me in a negative light. If anything, if you lie or exaggerate, you always do it for the opposite purpose!"

"It should also be perfectly identifiable, so that there are no doubts about his identity, even if you have to modify the personal details of the characters as you always do. You always do that, it wouldn't be credible if you used their real names," I continued.

"And how can I do that?"

"For example, you could include the detail of the invention of non-deformable tires by your client's father. The news of Dunlop recognizing the real paternity of what he believed to be his own invention has been reported by many newspapers in America. That way, they will understand that it's really him. We should also make them believe that they no longer have anything to fear from the documents," I further suggested, thinking aloud.

"The destruction, right?" Holmes replied, looking into my eyes as if it were now a matter concerning only the two of us.

"Exactly: the whole for the part!" I followed him, almost without letting him finish.

"What does that mean?" John asked again.

"Everything burned, everything destroyed, not just the documents that incriminated him but also those that were supposed to protect him. You find a way, Watson, you're the writer!" Holmes urged.

"And we have to act quickly: The news must reach them before they have time to organize a new expedition. And I would also advance the timeline of the whole story, pretending that it happened years ago, as you always do for your literary reasons," I added.

"I understand. The issue of time is what worries me the most: as fast as I can write, maybe without even having Arthur review the drafts, as I always do, I know that the editor has already finalized the contents of the next two issues of the Strand. I'm afraid we won't come out until after the summer," John informed us.

"That's not a problem," I intervened. "We will leak the news to the newspapers here in England, and Holmes will issue a warrant in the USA against those three for murder. When the authorities find out that they are dead, they will close the case, but in the meantime, word of the murder will reach those who need to know. Your story, in a few months, will be the final seal."

"Mhm. One more thing," Holmes added. "To make the death believable, we'll need to seek the help of some coroner friends. We need the body of an unrecognizable and undocumented drowning victim, along with the collaboration of a trusted friend who will identify him as Fred Thomson. I believe Prendegast can assist us in this matter. Besides knowing me well, I'm certain of his willingness and discretion, especially if I explain that it's a matter of life or death."

"To summarize, John," I concluded, "I recommend five points: One, act quickly to secure that poor man as soon as possible; two, make him identifiable, even under a pseudonym, without any room for doubt; three, convince the reader that Fred Thomson, or whatever name you'll use, is irreversibly deceased; four, be persuasive in making them believe that all the documents have been destroyed; five, lead them to believe that the destruction of the documents predates the crackdown carried out by the American secret services against the surviving members of the KKK. Is everything clear?"

"Crystal clear, Mary. Crystal clear," John replied, disciplined as always and rightly understanding the importance of his role in the successful outcome of the whole affair, while Holmes smiled and mimicked the gesture of applauding me.

I bowed to express my gratitude.

6.   From Mary's Diary

London, March 16, 1891

It's night. John has gone to bed exhausted and a little tipsy, both from the evening and the drinks. I told him I would join him soon, but I'm so excited, almost thrilled, about the role I had in this latest adventure that I can't imagine going to sleep without putting my impressions into writing. Even though half asleep, John made some observations about the "strange" connection he noticed between Holmes and me. "As if you know each other more than one would think, given your limited encounters." Perceptive, without a doubt. I think Dr. Watson has always underestimated himself.

A great connection, indeed. That's what disturbed me. In a positive way, I mean. At least, I think so. My heart was pounding, and my temples throbbed when we exchanged banter as if there were no one else. When thoughts formed simultaneously, and words couldn't catch up because they were so fast. And there was John, lagging a bit behind: attentive, meticulous, nitpicky, taking note of everything, but I could read the astonishment and surprise on his face with every turn. Then he would light up: he understood! But immediately after, a new task, a new obscure statement to comprehend, to clarify. What an effort, poor dear!

I have to be careful not to let our affinity with Holmes leak out so much. We need to be cautious. I don't want to make John jealous, and above all, I don't want him to think that I don't appreciate his qualities. Holmes is entertaining, stimulating, but a life with him would be unbearable, utterly devoid of the sweetness, tenderness, and emotional stability that are the characteristics of my husband, without whom I might risk becoming heartless.

THE RED LAMP

1.   The Incident

The woman staggered slightly, walking through the crowd with a vacant expression: young, extremely pale, poorly dressed, with a desperate look. She stopped for a moment before resuming a seemingly aimless, almost random ambling. Those who saw her later said she seemed to sway, with an empty gaze and a stunned expression, wearing worn-out clothes and an unsuitable shawl for the season. Suddenly, she slowly slipped, collapsing to the ground for no apparent reason, like a flower cut at its stem. Some people nearby moved away, either scared or perhaps to avoid inconvenience, but a middle-aged woman let out a scream and rushed to her aid, assisted by a gentleman who knelt beside her. The usual commotion that occurs in such cases followed until someone finally had the sense to raise their arm and stop a passing carriage:

"Take her to the hospital, coachman! She's alive and breathing, but she probably won't regain consciousness."

"Sure. And who's going to pay for the ride? She doesn't have a purse or wallet!"

"I'll pay for the ride," replied an elderly gentleman with an angry face and a heavy cane in his hand. "Here's a shilling, but if you don't hurry, I'll pay the rest with my cane. Move!"

"All right, all right, I'm going. Look at that ugly face. I bet she's Jewish. And she might die in the carriage, struggling to breathe, and dirtying my seats. It's always happening to me."

"Move, I said!!"

"I'm going, I'm going..."

The carriage departed, although not at full speed, and soon turned onto a side street. The coachman was bitter and, to tell the truth, he had half a mind to find an alley where he could drop the girl off and be rid of her, defying the old gentleman. Just as he was about to turn, he caught sight of a red lamp outside a house near the corner.

"A doctor! That's some luck! Stop, boys; let's stop here and make a good impression too! Hey, people in the house! Doctor! Is there a doctor here?"

The door opened, and John and I rushed out.

"You're the doctor, right? I have this girl here, doctor, she fainted on the street, and I'm afraid she won't make it to the hospital alive, doctor. I can't have her dying in my carriage; it's bad luck! Can you take care of her, right?"

John pushed him aside with a shove, not even uttering a word, and opened the door. He saw a worn-out girl, extremely pale, very poorly dressed, shoes almost falling apart, who looked exhausted.

"Give me a hand to bring her inside, at least."

"Sure, gov, right with you, here, I'll take her from this side. with that face I just hope that apart from being miserable, she's not a Jew. What filthy people! Coming here and taking our jobs!"

"At most, they take away your beer," my husband interrupted him, sternly. "Put her on the couch. And now, get out of here!"

"But of course," the man replied, all pleased. "All this trouble for a dirty Jew..."

"Keep in mind that even Jesus Christ was a dirty Jew. Try to think about it once in a while," I said to him, opening the door. The man hesitated, with wide-eyed astonishment.

"Ma'am, I really hope you don't let slip a blasphemy like that in front of your parish vicar, or else..."

He didn't finish his sentence because the door slammed shut an inch away from his beet-red nose.

"As if I would ever think of going to that pompous fatso, a proper friend for that ignorant racist. What do you think, John? Do you want hot water or towels?"

My husband was kneeling in front of the girl, diligently examining and auscultating her with experienced hands. He poured a drop of brandy between her lips, grabbed her wrist, checked her cheeks, and gently turned her eyelids, silently observing her. Then he stood up and reassured me.

"Nothing fatal or dangerous, I believe. I think it's the effects of prolonged malnutrition and excessive exertion: She fainted from hunger and exhaustion. In a word, she's sick from poverty. But she'll recover."

"Where... where am I?" she whispered with a barely audible voice.

"Among friends, dear, and everything is fine. Dr. Watson here says you'll be okay. But how long have you been walking? You must be tired."

"Since... since this morning."

"In this weather! And dressed like that. And how long since you've eaten?"

A bitter smile appeared on her poor face, as if resurfacing after such a long time that finding the way back wasn't easy.

"Three, four days..."

"Good heavens! Theresa! Where has that blessed girl gone! Here she is: Quickly, warm up that leftover broth from dinner. And help me take this poor girl to the children's room. She'll rest there tonight; there's no way we can send her away. Right, John?"

"Undoubtedly, dear. There's nothing else to be done, of course. We'll discuss the details later."

2.   From Mary's Diary

London, March 22, 1891

This morning, John was overwhelmed with work and had to leave very early to visit three patients who are causing him great concern. As he left, he entrusted me with the task of speaking to the girl when she woke up: "By now, listening to poor people has become your specialty," he said, laughing and kissing me at the doorstep. However, the girl slept for a long time, completely exhausted as she obviously was. This gave me some time to have a serious talk with that scatterbrained Theresa. That woman has always driven me crazy since she started working for us, after I had to dismiss the even more disastrous Mary Jane. Making the roast too well done or serving half-cooked potatoes at the table can be attributed to inexperience and can be tolerated. But when she confuses salt with sugar, resulting in abhorrently flavored morning coffee, or when she returns from grocery shopping with only half of the items on the list, then it's either sheer incompetence or a concentration problem due to personal problems. So I spoke to her very directly and asked her to be honest with me: Theresa denied having any problems, but stating it while twisting her hands and staring insistently out the window, which is not the best way to convince your listener. She's definitely hiding something, and I need to understand what it is or simply fire her. We certainly can't go on like this or we'll all end up poisoned.

3.   Like a Wounded Animal

I had just finished speaking with Theresa when the girl from the previous evening appeared before me, with an intimidated expression and downcast eyes, still wrapped in the dirty rags she was wearing. I practically forced her to have a hearty breakfast, with one of the cakes that Mrs. Hudson continues to send us regularly every week, and then I waited. I knew that offering her money, decent clothes, or any kind of help at that moment might be useless and perhaps even make her run away. I simply asked her to wait before immediately leaving as she claimed she wanted to do, and instead, keep me company while I embroidered, as I felt very lonely when John was at work: that's what I told her.

I observed her in silence, not taking the initiative first. There she was, huddled in a corner, perched on the edge of a chair like a wounded animal, with sad eyes and a gloomy expression. Slowly she gathered her courage, started talking to me, and I listened to her story.

"My name is Rachel. I am Jewish, as that cab driver told you. I was half asleep, but I heard what he said."

"What that brute said, dear, is as interesting to me as the stock quotes from Antwerp, and God knows I care very little about economics. Whether you're Jewish or Muslim, what does it matter to me?"

"Not everyone thinks like you."

"Yes, there are many idiots out there. Now, I may not be a genius, but I fail to see the correlation between your being Jewish and the indisputable fact that you wandered aimlessly for days until you collapsed unconscious. How did it come to this, my dear?" I asked touching her arm.

She let out a deep sigh and then launched into one of the most common, yet horrifying, stories I have ever heard. She lived in the degraded neighborhoods of the East End, in those alleys filled with overcrowded hovels where thousands of desperate people pay a fortune to English landlords to cram dozens of them into a single room. She, her father, and her mother had lived relatively well, considering the circumstances, until a few months ago, when her father, who had always worked in the textile industry, fell ill, ended up in the hospital, and eventually died.

"He had bladder cancer, they told us. It was terrible. He suffered tremendously, and we didn't have the money to treat him. He screamed in pain, in the end."

I shuddered at the thought of that death without help, in a filthy overcrowded room, without even the money for some relief from the pain. Rachel must have noticed my distress because she quickly tried to change the subject, and I had to insist for her not to leave, as she was about to do.

"You've told me too much, or too little. I need to know what happened to you/ True, it's none of my business, but last night we welcomed you and took responsibility for you. At this point, you don't think I'll let you go back walking the streets until you collapse again, do you? Sit down and tell me everything. Right now."

She obediently sat down, her eyes lowered, once again empty, filled only with despair.

"I knelt outside the textile factory asking to take my father's place: They felt sorry for me, it seems, and took me in. It was a good job: we worked twelve hours a day, even on Saturdays, may God forgive me. I couldn't even respect the Sabbath. But gradually, I began to suspect something. Maybe it's just an idea, but I found out that two other workers, a man and a woman, died of bladder cancer in previous years. I may be ignorant, but I became afraid that those things, those paints, could be harmful. You, being the wife of a doctor, do you think it's nonsense?"

"I honestly don't know. But did you ask questions?"

"I did more than that. I started connecting how long those people had been handling paints, and I discovered that the three deaths, including my father, were the ones who had been in contact with that stuff the longest. That's when the workshop manager told me to quit if I didn't want to be fired."

"But you kept going, and they fired you."

"There was no need. Two weeks ago, the workshop manager called me into his office, closed the door, and I knew what it meant. It had happened to other girls, and without realizing it, I grabbed a letter opener from his desk. And when he approached me, I threatened to hit him and ran away. The next morning, they didn't let me back to work. They fired me."

"Scoundrel!" I muttered to myself.

And I made a note to ask her the name of that gentleman. I thought Clara would undoubtedly find a way to make him change his behavior. But Rachel continued speaking, with a subdued, almost mechanical voice, and the more she spoke, the tighter my heart clenched. Since her father's death, their financial situation had worsened significantly, as her wages were half of her father's, and hunger had entered their lives. It was tough to work so hard and eat so little, but she always appeared cheerful to her poor mother. She wanted to seem happy, to save her worrying and by saving on everything and often fasting, pretending not to be hungry, she had always managed to keep her mother healthy without making her realize how really dramatic their situation was. But when she lost her job everything collapsed, the precarious balance had been irreparably broken.

There was only one solution, one she knew as all the other girls knew it: but she would never do that. Death would be better, but could she let her mother die too? That's why she hadn't told her anything and had gone out every day for two weeks, as if going to work, searching for a job all over London, walking for hours until her shoes were worn out, until that last day when even hope had vanished, and she had simply walked and walked without a reason until she fainted.

"One thing is certain," I told her when she finished. "You're not moving from here until I've talked to my husband. We'll send a note to your mother to reassure her and let her know where you are; she'll be worried."

4.   Two problems: one of the heart and one of paints

That evening, Theresa's suitcase near the door foretold a storm. She was in the kitchen, wringing her hands and pacing back and forth, just as she had done that morning. She rushed towards me, almost in tears.

"Please forgive me, ma'am, please forgive me. I can't stay here and work; you've seen how unwell I am. My mind is always somewhere else."

"It's not that noticeable," I thought without saying it, while comforting her with an affectionate gesture.

"You've been so kind to me... and you even asked me what was happening. Well, my fiancé left me, that's what. Without even telling me why, from one day to the next. I can't work; I need some time for myself. You don't mind, do you?"

What could I say? I let her go to her own home, to her mother, presumably to cry on her bed, like the silly girl she was. Strange, however, I thought: her love story was a daily topic of discussion in my house, and not once had a cloud been reported to me. Of course, she was a silly girl, but attentive to the nuances of her handsome boyfriend's behavior. Nevertheless, I reassured her, telling her that I could manage without her for a few days and that I was expecting news. And as soon as Theresa left, as swift as the wind or, rather, like rain clouds driven by the wind, given her copious tears, John came back home.

"How are my patient and my beautiful nurse?" he said, gallantly.

I reassured him and gave him a complete account of what had happened, including Theresa's escape.

"Well," he said calmly, lighting his pipe, "that works out perfectly for now. Rachel can stay here until she recovers, especially since Theresa has left, and her room is available. For what little that scatterbrain was doing, Rachel can certainly give you a hand here at home."

"Do you know that she asked me if it bothered us that she's Jewish, given that we're Christians?"

My husband's face darkened.

"I understand many things, but not this. Hatred in the name of God. Yet the city is full of it."

154

"Indeed. I remember that passage in Voltaire's *Philosophical Dictionary* when Christ returns and wanders among the pyres of the victims of religious wars, weeping. The world is full of idiots."

"And scoundrels who take advantage of it, my dear little Voltairean. Since you started taking care of the disadvantaged, you've become quite revolutionary, you know?"

"Hands off, Doctor. Rachel might catch us, and I am a married woman."

"To me!"

"But married! And a serious wife doesn't let loose in the parlor at this hour. Instead, what do you think of Rachel's suspicion? Could those paints be toxic?"

John became thoughtful. I knew that when it came to medicine, he stopped joking immediately and took things seriously. He stuck the pipe in his mouth and furrowed his brow, deep in thought.

"Well, I confess I've read something here and there. Not proper articles or significant research, mind you, but some reports of clinical cases: I can't remember exactly where. But... yes, here it is: Young Noggart, at dinner at the club the other night, told me that he's in contact with a German researcher working on that."

"Oh, dear! It would be so wonderful of you to delve into the matter... just imagine if Rachel were right! After all, it's an investigation, and you're the expert in this field. I'll also take care of consoling the afflicted, as you say when you tease me, but I'm certainly not a woman of action, let alone of science."

5.   From Mary's Diary

London, March 29, 1891

I've had too much to do to update the diary in the past few days. Meanwhile, Rachel is settling into the house, almost taking Theresa's place, who is still living with her mother. She helps me with the chores, playing a subdued but increasingly indispensable role. We agreed on a salary for her, although she's more like a friend than an employee. She rushes to give the money to her mother every week. She appears calmer but still deeply affected. As John says, it takes time to recover from severe malnutrition, and it's not just about good food. Those who go through that infernal experience remain deeply affected and lose the will to care for themselves for a long time... By the way, recently I went to visit Theresa, whom I found with her family, still in a river of tears. Her lover has left her, as we knew, refusing to see her and not responding to her letters—a total and brutal breakup that the poor girl cannot understand or comprehend the reason for.

6.   Research and Deductions

A few days after our conversation about paints being possibly toxic, while we were having breakfast John showed me, with quite a satisfied look on his face, a letter from Germany: it was from the German doctor he had been told about. He had sent him a telegram, asking for information about his work and explaining the reason for it, and the doctor kindly replied immediately by mail. John explained to me that it was a certain Dr. Ludwig Rehn, a prominent figure in Frankfurt. He also had the suspicion that certain paints, especially aniline, could be related to the onset of bladder cancer: He was studying it, but he didn't have any conclusive data yet. Also, John pointed out, biting his extinguished pipe thoughtfully, how could one prove that the dyes used were the toxic ones? And how could one test the dilutions?

"Well, of course, if the percentage of sick workers was abnormal compared to the rest of the population, then... yes, it could be a way to show the connection" he concluded with a sparkle in his eyes.

That's when Rachel interrupted us, very excited:

"Doctor, but I already have some evidence. You see, before I got fired, I had my nose in a bit of everything, the lady knows it, to the point that I was threatened. I noticed that many dye workers were fired after a few years, and asking around in town, I discovered that several of them died of cancer, like my father, many years after having to leave the factory."

"That's not enough. There could be many other causes and they could be mixed up with each other."

"So what could be done, then? I don't understand, but maybe we could manage to get a list of the workers involved, year by year, don't you think?" I intervened.

"Indeed, Mary, if we had that, we could check how long they worked there, and then see from a distance if they got sick..."

"A great idea, dear. Of course, compiling those lists won't be easy... unless you ask for them, please."

"What do you mean?"

"Perhaps you could say that you're conducting research on the harmful effects of tobacco or excessive drinking, and that you need those lists for that purpose. And that you would like to randomly visit some of those individuals to find out how much they drink. Do you think management would agree? Maybe in exchange for a mention and a word of thanks in the article you'll publish?"

John started getting restless in his chair: it was clear that the idea had struck him.

"If you think so, I believe I can put in a good word with Mr. Richardson, the owner. A friend of mine knows his secretary well," I added.

How well and, above all, in what way Clara knew him, I preferred to keep to myself. John locked himself in his study to prepare a research outline, all fired up by the idea, while I got ready to visit Clara to ask for her help, and Rachel left to visit her mother: thus, our quiet breakfast turned into a frantic morning.

Clara doesn't live near me, which is fortunate if you consider that sometimes I hide at her home so that John can't find me out, so I took a cab to go and see her. But in the midst of the traffic, just as my hansom cab got stuck between a fruit cart that was losing its load and a four-wheeler whose driver was hurling the worst insults at mine, among the crowd bustling on the sidewalk, I saw Thomas, Theresa's handsome boyfriend, disheveled and with a worried look on his face, walking briskly despite being the object of shoves and protests. They say curiosity is a woman's trait, and maybe it's a silly thing, but I couldn't help but wonder what he was doing at that hour and where he was going with such determination.

Without thinking twice, I got out of the hansom, using the excuse that it was blocked in the traffic, and started following him from a distance. During rush hour, nobody would notice a respectable lady walking briskly, so thankfully, I could follow him even without a disguise. It's not that I wanted to meddle between Theresa and her lover but at that point, I felt involved enough in the silly affairs of my maid to feel entitled to poke my nose in. It could be that Tom had a lover, and simply for that reason, he abruptly left poor Theresa - disgraceful but human. Why hadn't he told her, though? And why the hurried demeanor? I noticed that he looked back from time to time, as if he thought he were being followed: Fortunately, Theresa had shown him to me, with great detail and multiple times, only from the window while she waited for him, and she had never officially introduced him to me, so I highly doubted the boy would take notice of me.

Everything changed suddenly when he turned at a crossing and entered a nearly deserted park. Was he taking a shortcut? Did he have an appointment with a woman and was simply running late? I hesitated for a moment, and it was a good thing I did because I saw him join a man who was waiting for him under a large oak tree in a somewhat secluded spot. A dense hedge provided me with a good vantage point that was invisible to them. I was too far away to distinguish the words they exchanged, but the tone seemed to be rising quickly until two thugs jumped out from behind a bush and held Tom while the first one beat him mercilessly. I was frozen: There was no way I could intervene, and there was no one around to ask for help, let alone a police officer. Besides, the scene lasted only a few seconds: the three ruffians disappeared, leaving that poor fellow nearly unconscious on the ground.

"Oh my God, Thomas, look at what they've done to you. Your poor nose... there must be something broken, no, a couple of cracked ribs. Those ruffians must have had brass knuckles."

"Who... who are you? A nurse?"

"My husband is a doctor, so I know a thing or two."

He sat up, swollen from the blows and dazed, with a black eye.

"But do you know me? How do you know my name? Just leave me alone, please, leave me alone. I fell, leave me alone."

"But what the devil are you saying? I saw the whole scene. They set you up and beat you like blacksmiths. Listen, young man, you have two choices. One is to leave and get beaten up - or worse - next time, the other is to trust me. I can help you."

"No one can," he replied gloomily, looking down.

"And why not? You're not the first one to fall victim to loan sharks."

He jumped in surprise.

"Oh, come on! It doesn't take Sherlock Holmes to deduce these things. But tell me, did you leave your girlfriend for this reason?"

Honestly, I believe that this sentence would have knocked him to the ground more than the blows he had received earlier, if he hadn't already been sitting.

"You're a witch! A fairy! How do you know these things?"

I looked at him with compassion. A man who doesn't have a watch, despite having a deformed buttonhole where he used to attach the chain, and who doesn't wear the gold pin his girlfriend gave him on his lapel aside from giving me a headache with the whole pitiful story, is someone who has had to sell even the last valuable item he had: the state of his clothes, tasteful but neglected, indicated that the collapse of his fortune had been recent, and the scene I witnessed was a classic warning from that kind of people.

"Forget about that and answer me instead. Look, next time they'll kill you: they'd rather lose the money than their reputation, that's how they think, and those who don't pay disappear in the Thames. You wouldn't be the first."

The young man stared at me wide-eyed, and I thought about what Holmes felt when he used his deductions to impress clients. In my case, it wasn't intentional, but the effect was extraordinary.

"I truly don't know who you are or how you know these things, but at this point, I might as well tell the truth. Well, considering what I have to lose... it's like you said: I owe a huge sum to those guys, and I have no chance of recovering it unless I rob a bank. I'm as good as dead, I know it."

"How much?"

"Fifty guineas. Don't look at me like that, I know how much fifty guineas are. I could work for a whole year and not earn half of it... but I didn't gamble it away. My mother was very ill and there was no chance of curing her. Doctors, medicine, hospitals... for years. I got into debt, one thing then another. You seem to know the rest."

"And your girlfriend?

"Theresa!" He wrung his hands, unintentionally imitating his girlfriend's gesture. "My God... how is she? What will she do? But I couldn't do otherwise. I can't tie her to a person like me, dragging her into poverty and trouble. She'll be unhappy for a while, then maybe she'll find someone else... what am I saying, my God, what am I saying!"

Seeing a beaten man in tears on the ground, comforted by a young lady, is not exactly what one considers a dignified spectacle. Therefore, to protect public decency, I helped Thomas to his feet and scolded him severely.

"You're a fool through and through, that's for sure. You deserve a good beating, but you've already had enough. Follow me and keep quiet. No, tell me first: What's your religion? Anglican? Fine. Methodist? Even better. Come on, let's get into that carriage, and quickly, please. You wouldn't want to compromise me!"

From St. Paul's, where we went in the cab it was easy to make our way to the river and reach the Salvation Army headquarters. The young man followed me, ashamed, a few steps behind, and I didn't mind having someone watch my back in those streets, even if it was daytime.

At the entrance, I marched decisively towards the girls in uniform and curtly asked for Sergeant Anna Woodrock. They didn't bat an eye and immediately sent for her. Something had served me well to marry a former officer and be the daughter of another: with certain people, all it took was giving firm orders to be obeyed. I had met Anna in the early cases I had followed and I appreciated the efforts she and her colleagues made to improve things in the slums. I also understood that a rigid military organization achieved better results in certain environments than simple charity offered with kindness by worthy individuals. However, as I had often told Anna, I felt that was not my way: too rigid and unbending, too strict in its discipline and predetermined methods. I preferred to move in complete autonomy, aligning myself with Catholics, socialists, anarchists, and Methodists. Whether it was right or not, Someone wiser than me would tell me at the end of my days.

I didn't have much to explain to my friend, who received me and the boy in a reserved room where they had just finished singing hymns. Thomas collapsed completely, recounting his misfortunes, his attempts to escape from an impossible situation, his despair. Poor boy, he didn't even ask for help anymore. He had hit rock bottom and simply spoke in a flat voice, staring at the floor as if convinced that nothing and no one could do anything for him.

"Well, well," my friend reflected aloud, "it's a bad situation. Certainly, no one could put together fifty guineas just to give to those scoundrels. But you have an idea, Mary. I know you well enough to know that you wouldn't have brought him to me otherwise."

"Weren't you the one telling me about the new missions you're thinking of starting in the colonies? In Australia, for example? It wouldn't cost much to make the boy disappear for a few days and buy a couple of tickets to Australia. And you would have two valuable recruits for the Army down there; he is a hard worker."

"Two?!" Thomas managed to add, looking up at me, his eyes filled with a spark of hope.

"Surely you don't think I went through all this trouble just for you, right? Go immediately to that poor girl. For a few days, the loan sharks will leave you alone before pouncing on you again. Throw yourself at her feet, tell her everything, and ask her to marry you. The only thing that bothers me about this affair is that she won't be able to come and work as a maid for me anymore."

"Mrs. Watson!"

"A brilliant deduction, boy, although a bit late. Now, get moving."

7.   From Mary's Diary

London, March 30, 1891
And that's done, I repeated to myself, satisfied and with a hint of pride, as I finally went to see Clara. The lovebirds will secretly set sail for the colonies in four days, and the loan sharks in Clerkenwell will be left with nothing. I informed Clara of the latest events, and she congratulated me on the affair of the loving couple, saying that I'm becoming more and more like Sherlock

Holmes, although she wasn't entirely sure if it was a compliment. Then we devised our plan to get Richardson to authorize John's search. *Clara is certain that a simple note to the director's secretary will be enough, without any additional comments. She knows that they won't be able to refuse her. She quickly wrote it down and immediately called a courier to deliver it the same day. If John acts quickly to send his request, he can expect a very fast response.*

Clara is truly my secret weapon.

8.   New Problems

Two days later, while we were having breakfast, the mailman rang the doorbell. Rachel was still not in sight, and John rushed to answer it himself. He came back immediately, all excited, holding an invitation to visit the textile factory. He explained that the day before, he had sent a simple letter to the director requesting collaboration for a scientific analysis.

"Great timing," commented my naive husband.

I hope he never finds out that the director's secretary is a frequent guest at Clara's dinners, and that a certain influence in his choices was the result of an emotionally charged evening at her house. I spent a good twenty minutes celebrating with John and listening to his ideas and plans for the research that could unfold at the factory, after looking into the lists of current and past workers. It seemed important to congratulate him and offer him some subtle suggestions to assist him. But something was troubling me. Where was Rachel? Why didn't she join us for breakfast? I apologized and went to look for her, and as I feared, something was really wrong. The girl was locked in her room, crying helplessly: Her mother had disappeared.

"She had been acting strange for a few weeks," Rachel told me between sobs. "She went out less and less, cried in secret, and didn't want to see anyone. Could she have found out that I was laid off, even though I pretend otherwise? Today, when I went to her house, as I do from time to time to give her some food and the money you give me, I found out that she left home two days ago. The neighbors simply haven't seen her, and there's no note or message at home. She didn't take anything with her. What could have happened? Oh, my God!"

Without wasting any time, I took off like a rocket, with Rachel struggling to keep up behind me (she was still very weak), to go and take a look at her house, something I hadn't done. What I saw would horrify anyone. None of us realizes the abyss of horror and misery hidden beneath the fragile surface of a presumably humane society. In the depths of the destitute, there is only hell. Passing through foul-smelling alleyways where naked children chased each other, crying, encountering people dazed by hunger and hardship, discovering corners so dark that one wonders if the sunlight ever touched them, we arrived at one of the shanties among many others. It seemed to stand only because it was propped up by similar ones, like a group of drunks leaning on each other. We climbed up stairs that were kept somewhat clean by the heroic attempts of those who lived there, but with floors so worn and walls so threadbare that they were desolate to behold. And we entered an apartment shared by a small crowd of people: old people, children, young women with vacant and absent gazes, many of them pregnant, but with faces very different from the calm and sweet ones I had known in many friends. There, Rachel and her mother had been reduced to living in that cramped three-room apartment inhabited by almost twenty people, surviving on the girl's meager wages, when she had them. I asked everyone about Rachel's mother, but I got very few answers. One day she was simply gone, that's all. Her poor trunk with her belongings, her rags, was still there, and we had to be careful not to let on that she had disappeared, or those miserable rags would be instantly divided among those desperate souls. None of them paid any attention to that poor woman, and probably not to anyone or anything else that wasn't strictly necessary for survival. I left there perplexed: Where were the clues, the leads that Sherlock Holmes would have sought and, of course, found? The witnesses, the traces? I had to find another way to find her. I returned home defeated and worried about the results of my investigations, careful not to let these feelings show in front of Rachel.

Meanwhile, John had gone to the textile factory where he was received with great kindness and given access to the records of all the workers. He immediately realized that the task ahead would be long and complicated as the names were not divided by department but were recorded in order of hiring date. The department they were assigned to was written next to the name, but in case of job changes or transfers, the previous department was crossed out with a line, and the new one was annotated without a date.

Furthermore, the register of dismissals or retirements was separate from the register of hirings. All this made it very difficult to reconstruct the personal journey of each worker in the company, their time of employment, and especially their activities in the paint department. On the other hand, the plan to visit all potential poisoning victims depended on being able to compile a list to identify them - he couldn't proceed randomly. So he resigned himself to dedicating the necessary time to this task and started patiently copying those records, page by page, to cross-reference the data at home at a later time. Working a couple of hours a day, which he deemed possible to spare from his professional activities, he estimated that he would have to copy names for at least a week.

While he was copying, he noticed the presence of children in the factory who were certainly younger than seven. However, when he checked the latest pages of the records, he realized that there was no one who, at the time of hiring, was younger than eight, the legal limit. It was clear that they were either working off the books or their data had been falsified - and to think that there were inspectors specifically tasked with monitoring child labor violations. It was evident, though not easily provable, that they had been corrupted. When he returned home, he told me everything, unsure if he was angrier or sadder about the state of affairs.

In the afternoon, before returning to Rachel's house to continue my investigations, I organized myself to mobilize all the resources at our disposal. I summoned all my "adventuresses" to Clara's house: Polly, the Italian seamstress; Anna, my Salvation Army friend; Louise, the sailor's girlfriend; Annie, the dressmaker; Jenny, the cunning spy, and of course, Amina, our aspiring legal consultant.

"Girls," I began, "I absolutely need you. I can't do this alone. I need to find a woman, the elderly mother of a new friend, who hardly speaks any English because she's

Jewish and only knows Yiddish. She left home without leaving any indication a couple of days ago. But she couldn't have gone very far because she's not well and doesn't have much stamina. I think Anna and her Army can take care of hospitals and shelters, Polly can spread the word in the docks and the Italian neighborhood. Louise will handle the port, and Annie will do her best with her salesgirl friends downtown. Jenny has many other colleagues she can ask for help, and Amina will come with me to comb the neighborhood where she disappeared and the train stations."

So, without further hesitation, we all got to work, dispersing throughout the city, with an agreement to immediately report any discoveries or clues to Clara, who would stay at home. After a couple of hours of wandering aimlessly in the neighborhood, Amina and I found ourselves in front of Paddington Station. We entered to ask if anyone had noticed her, without much conviction, as until that moment it seemed like we were searching for an invisible woman. However, we were fortunate because the ticket collector we approached not only had noticed her but had even had an altercation with her before realizing that the strange old lady definitely needed help.

"She seemed a bit daft to me. Can you imagine that, expressing herself in a largely incomprehensible language, she asked me for a discount on the ticket price without even having an idea of where she was going? She told me, or at least that's what I understood, that she wanted to go anywhere as long as she could pay less. At that point, I realized that something was off, so I called the railway police, and they immediately took her to Bow Street."

It was too late to go to the police to speak to her, but the important thing was knowing that she was safe for the time being. Before returning home to reassure Rachel, Amina and I went to Clara's to report the discovery and give instructions for the others to stop their searches. Then I went back home to deliver the news to Rachel and John.

9.   From Mary's Diary

London, April 2, 1891

It took some persuasion to convince Rachel to wait until tomorrow to retrieve her mother. John helped me by suggesting that he accompany us, thus leveraging his authority and reputation with the police. I like the fervor with which my husband is approaching the whole situation of Rachel, her father, and her mother. The dedication he puts into trying to determine if there is a provable link between the illnesses of those men and women and the paints they used at work has nothing to do with the perspective of my revolutionary friends who pit the exploited workers against the exploited masters, it rather stems from his deep sense of morality. John is a conservative, yes, but he is also fundamentally honest and very sensitive to another conflict, that between a dishonest employer and a worker victimized by dishonesty. I have discovered in him the strength of his calling as a doctor, who cares for the patients in his practice as well as rights the wrongs of victims of criminal behavior with his friend Holmes. He observes, recognizes, hypothesizes, intervenes, and verifies the effects of his intervention. Perhaps, at the beginning of all this I tried to gratify him as a stimulus to influence him and have him by my side, but now, seeing him in action, I am truly

*enthusiastic about him and increasingly happy that he is the man
of my life.*

10.   The Clinician's Eye

The next morning, we woke up early. Rachel had been up
for a while, assuming she had even slept. We settled for a quick
breakfast so as not to prolong the girl's agony.

"You know, John, I was thinking about this story
that has engaged both of us," I began while sipping my
tea. "I realized that you and I are much more similar than
it may seem at first glance. I used to think we were
complementary, and in many ways, I still believe that, but
I have discovered that we also share a deep affinity."

"Well, we are certainly both honest and generous, I
believe," he replied.

"Yes, of course, but I'm referring to something we
have in common with your friend Holmes, which I would
describe as a reparative vocation: We cannot stand
injustices. When faced with an injustice, it eats away at
us, and we cannot find peace until we have tried, at least
tried, to set things right."

"Well, I am a doctor, and that applies to my
profession too. After all, illness is an anomaly to be
repaired. I do relate to that, yes."

"That's fundamentally what justifies my social
commitment, you know? In this case, besides helping
Rachel and her mother, I would love to seek justice for the
wrongs suffered by those male and female workers. If

there is a link, that is... But how would Holmes handle a case like this? How could he gather firsthand information without raising suspicion among the suspects?"

"He would use the Irregulars, obviously. But Holmes has disappeared lately, nobody knows where he is, and the Irregulars don't have much sympathy for me."

"What if I told you that I also have a small but highly efficient group of collaborators, or rather, female collaborators? We call ourselves the 'Adventuresses of Regent Street,' named after one of them, who lives in an apartment we consider our base. Out of gratitude, affection, and solidarity, they are absolutely loyal to me. Could they assist you in your investigations into the connections between paints and illnesses?"

"I'm not sure how; I need to think about it. But thank you, thank you for the opportunity, but most of all, thank you for shedding light on what you do without me... After discovering that you're not visiting nonexistent relatives but dedicating yourself heart and soul to social activities, after seeing you in action, matching wits with Holmes in his reasoning, today I find out that you have a small army of helpers at your disposal, the 'Adventuresses.' I don't know what else to expect from you... perhaps at any moment I will learn that Mycroft has recruited you for the British Secret Service..."

"No, wait! The lead on this investigation is yours because I wouldn't know where to begin. I deal with small things, matters of the heart, small financial problems or trivial family conflicts. At most, neglected children in need of care and attention. Things that exclude manifestly violent behavior like assault or abuse, or actual crimes fall outside my scope. If I were to come across any of those, I would immediately turn to the police. But you, I see that you've become accustomed to dealing with situations which are more nearly criminal, and therefore, especially if you can do it without personally exposing yourself, you are the most suitable person to investigate Rachel's suspicions."

We interrupted the conversation, which was stretching on too long, and headed to the Bow Street police station, a place John was very familiar with, in a carriage. The station was connected to the adjacent premises of the local magistrate and had not only the usual holding cell but also other more comfortable rooms used as waiting areas or interrogation rooms.

It was in one of these rooms, decidedly more welcoming than the foul corner where she had been living lately, that we found Rachel's mother. She was wrapped in a blanket, lying on a military cot, dozing off. The police officers told us they were still trying to identify her, both because she was very confused and because none of them understood the language she spoke. They were still waiting for a rabbi who had offered to act as an interpreter but who hadn't been able to come yet due to other commitments. They said they had given her some food, and after eating, she lay down without causing any trouble, although she had been moaning all night. Thank goodness Dr. Watson had arrived; he would set everything right!

Rachel was deeply moved and happy at the same time to have found her mother safe and sound, after fearing the worst. She tried to wake her with an embrace, but the woman, upon opening her eyes and recognizing her daughter, turned away and started sobbing again. Rachel was devastated by that completely unexpected and incomprehensible reaction. I approached her to try and talk to her, gently asking what the problem was, but she didn't treat me any better than she did her daughter. She refused to even look at me and muttered something in her own language, barely audible:

"Prison, prison, better to stay in prison... Great dishonor..."

I had the idea to make another attempt, sensing that there might be an opening to get her to speak. However, I thought it would be appropriate to ask John and Rachel to leave us alone. I sat next to her on the cot, in silence, gently placing a hand on her shoulder. After a few minutes, it seemed that the physical contact had some effect, as her crying became less intense, and her breathing seemed more relaxed. I decided to try talking to her again, very slowly, choosing language I hoped she could understand.

"I deeply respect your pain, ma'am, which must be immense if you would prefer to stay in prison, as you mentioned. But I would like to tell you that, no matter how serious what has happened to you may be, we can try to find a solution together. My husband, the gentleman you saw here earlier, is a doctor, and together with me, we are willing to do everything to help you, especially if it concerns your health. And then there's your daughter, Rachel, whom I have recently met, truly a good girl. She cares about you deeply and would do anything to see you in a better state..."

The woman lifted her head and stared at me intensely.

"But it is she who brought dishonor to our family. I can no longer leave the house because of her" she said, regaining her voice and determination.

"But what has she done that is so grave?"

"It's been two months since she left her period! She's pregnant without a husband! She's a disgraceful woman!"

The truth suddenly appeared before me in all its clarity.

"Oh, God! How long has it been since you saw your daughter without clothes? Haven't you realized how much she weighs? How much she has become thin?"

Then I turned to my husband, who had remained nearby:

"John, come here, please! You need to explain something to this lady, with your authority as a doctor."

John approached, and I continued:

"You should tell her, if you don't mind, what happens to a female body when it goes below a certain weight limit. Listen to him, ma'am: It's a doctor speaking."

"Well, apart from weakness, fatigue, and easy exhaustion, the first thing is the suspension of the menstrual cycle," John said, putting on an overtly professional air.

"Do you understand? Your daughter is hungry and weak, so weak that her body is no longer functioning properly. It has nothing to do with pregnancy, let alone dishonor. You should be proud of your daughter, instead, for the courage she has shown towards her employers and her attachment to you, which made her not want to worry you and pretend that everything was fine, even when she lost her job! She went hungry for weeks to feed you, and that's why she lost her cycle!"

11.   From Mary's Diary

London, April 4, 1891
    The adventure of the past few days has had a fairly satisfying conclusion, even though John's research on the connections between paints and deadly diseases is progressing slowly and is far from leaving the realm of conjecture to enter the realm of certainty. But he is tenacious, and he will succeed[2]. And thanks to the combined efforts of my husband, with his determination, and my Adventuresses, with their imagination and spy skills, we have not only proved that underage workers were employed in the factory, contrary to the law but also that the factory director, Mr. Richardson, falsified documents and bribed officials to avoid being caught. That was enough to land him in jail, where I hope he will pay for all his sins, including, if there is evidence, causing the death of his workers.

    By the way, the foreman who abused the female workers and got Rachel fired has had a series of unfortunate accidents thanks to some of Clara's friends, that will make him reflect on his ungentlemanly behavior.

---

[2]   Watson was unable to directly prove what he was looking for. But it was certainly thanks to the clues he collected that Ludwig Rehn presented in 1895 the results of the first study linking paint and bladder cancer.

Rachel will stay with us permanently, taking Theresa's place, and since there is room, her mother will also come to live with us. Apparently, her Kosher cooking is unbeatable.

I am happy because my bond with John has grown even stronger: he is truly my preux chevalier without blemish or fear.

I would undoubtedly consider myself happy if a black cloud didn't constantly hang over my head: I always feel tired, too tired not to fear that my body is also fragile, like that of my poor mother. Consumption, this terrible word, is a curse that looms over the heads of my family members. Perhaps I should start taking care of myself as much as I try to do for others.

A final thought on the red lamp, the visible symbol displayed for all to see, representing John's constant readiness to help others and my affinity with him: How could I light a similar lamp in front of my door to attract my own destitutes?

THE FINAL PROBLEM

1. From Mary's Diary

London, April 21, 1891

Tonight I talked to John about the mission entrusted to me by the Cardinal: I will have to spend three or four days in Bristol, organizing a support group for the cases of extreme poverty among the dock workers. Essentially, I will be sharing the experiences from London and assisting in organizing the group. I'm leaving tomorrow. I feel a bit sorry for leaving John alone so often, and the idea of being away from home for several days worries me. This strange fatigue, which I dare not name, is relentless. However, talking to my husband reassures me: Ever since he found out about all my activities, we have complete understanding and support between us, even though I notice his concern for me, which, if it doesn't hinder me, I've discovered brings me immense pleasure. What woman doesn't love to be pampered a little?

London, April 25, 1891

Today, upon my return from Bristol, I had a terrible surprise. John had left for the Continent with Holmes. He left me a long and sweet letter explaining everything. Just last night, his friend came to our house and explained the situation he's in. As I already knew because Holmes himself had told me about it, for months he has been trying to corner a criminal mastermind so powerful, dangerous, and elusive that he is willing to risk everything to succeed. That man, a certain Professor Moriarty, confronted him and proposed an agreement that Holmes, being the man he is, refused.

Within a few hours, he faced two attempts on his life and refused to stay with us to avoid endangering John as well. A major operation is about to take place, thanks to Holmes's discoveries, but he has decided to silently decamp to Europe and wait there until the danger subsides and Moriarty is in prison. John, of course, has sided with him and accompanies him. I love him for this too, for his unwavering sense of honor and his inability to back down. I must admit, I am very worried. Holmes's adventures always involve a certain level of danger, but this time it's a matter of life or death. God forbid I regret agreeing to that mission in Bristol. To be the first to help others and then fail to help those closest to me, to not be by his side in moments of danger!

But on the other hand, what could I have done if I had been here, other than embrace him and give him my blessing for this adventure? Yet, it would have still been better than reading a letter and agonizing in anguish. I will talk to him about it, but I already know his response: "We are equals, you and I, and we love each other for this. We are incapable of standing idly by without trying to do something against evil. Do what you must do, as you allow me to do the same."

2. Exciting Anticipation

Instead of staying at home waiting, I decided to immerse myself in my work. The situation at the port and in the slums was under control, so I decided to return to Bristol, extending my stay there to finish the work I had only hastily completed. There was a particular family that had touched my heart, with a little girl of only ten who was seriously ill. She, too, had tuberculosis, the accursed plague that mows down young lives in their prime, denying happiness and a future. Was I speaking of my fear here, instead of compassion? But certainly, in the dark alleys and sunless corners, in the damp and overcrowded rooms, in the houses filled only with poverty and hunger, the Grim Reaper strikes without respite and without mercy. I understood my husband well, who considered him the enemy he had decided to fight all his life, even though he knew that at best he could only postpone losing his patients!

So I went to Bristol and spent several days with the Smiths, staying up nights to watch over the little girl together with her unfortunate mother. The heart-wrenching scenes I experienced every day, the desperate anguish of that family, which I shared wholeheartedly, perhaps helped me contain my own worries. In London, Rachel had orders to forward me any telegram that arrived, and not a day went by without me reading all the morning and evening editions, searching for news of a major crackdown on criminals and, in particular, Professor Moriarty. But the days passed, and everything remained silent.

A few days later, the inevitable happened, and the little girl was called to heaven. At least she fell asleep with a serene smile while perhaps dreaming of better things, even though her mother's screams and the scenes of pain I witnessed will forever be etched in my mind. I returned from Bristol with a heavy heart full of bitterness and anguished questions to which no one could ever provide me with answers.

At Paddington station, I received another blow.

"Evening Standard!" shouted a small newsboy at the exit. "Latest news! Extensive criminal gang arrested by the police! The infamous professor, the gang's leader, is on the run!"

I almost snatched a copy of the newspaper from his hands and gritted my teeth as I read the text: "*Just concluded,*" the article read, *"is one of the most brilliant operations ever executed by Scotland Yard against crime. We are pleased to emphasize that this success is primarily the result of the tireless work and acute intelligence of Inspector G. Lestrade, who coordinated the operations in the field. Over a hundred evildoers and outright criminals have been brought to justice, including many unsuspected individuals who sought refuge not in the alleys of the East End, but in the most renowned professional environments and even in banks and government offices. Only a few have escaped justice for now, particularly the head of this infamous organization, but the judicial machinery is at work, and well-informed sources tell us that investigators are already on the trail of the few fugitives."*

I crumpled that newspaper in anger. Where was Moriarty? Where was my husband? I understood perfectly well that John couldn't send me any news. If the criminal organization was so vast and Moriarty was still at large, any message could have been intercepted. Without even going home, I did the only thing that made sense: I went to Pall Mall to Mycroft Holmes's office.

The elder Holmes brother received me courteously, but with a worried look. A robust man with a plump face, he usually had a reassuring and kind appearance that concealed his acute intelligence and icy determination. But that time, what his face conveyed to me was concern and tension.

"Dear madam, I have no news, and I do not even know exactly where they are. My brother and your husband are traveling incognito, so they have not approached our agents in Europe, who are nevertheless all alerted to locate the professor and stop him at any cost. I believe he is also in Europe, on the trail of Watson and Sherlock, but I trust that with his astuteness, my brother will manage to elude the pursuit until it is Moriarty himself who is trapped by ours. All we can do is hope and wait: I will immediately communicate any news to you, and you can count on me for anything you may need."

I will remember those days forever. And those nights, spent with a heavy heart, waiting for news that I didn't know whether to fear or desire. Every ring of the bell, every knock on the door made me startle as if it were the call of the angel of death. I had never felt such sorrow in my life, and now I knew what my mother had felt when my father was in danger. As the daughter of a soldier, I knew well what my duty as a wife was: to wait, to endure, not to give in, and to always hope, at any cost.

And one night, it finally happened. I had not yet gone to bed when a messenger knocked to deliver a telegram from Switzerland. I opened it with trembling hands: it was from John.

"*A tragedy has occurred. Holmes and his mortal enemy have both fallen: He is dead; there is no more hope. The world is empty. I will return to London as soon as possible.*"

"Everything is over": this thought exploded in my brain as I stood in front of the fire, rereading the few lines on that yellow sheet of paper over and over again. I was incredulous: Deep down, I had always considered Sherlock Holmes to be immortal, invincible, an absolute hero with no possibility of defeat. And yet, he was just a man, as I had always known deep inside, but to discover it in this way, to have to face the truth so brutally, was a terrible disillusionment.

"*The world is empty*," my husband had written, and that was truly the sensation I felt, and that I experienced in the following two days, waiting for John. I had responded to him "*I am waiting for you. I love you.*" But there was no longer anyone standing between us and evil: the hero who had sacrificed his entire life to defend us. It was up to us now, I sensed that in my soul. Yet, the initial disbelief had given way to complete disillusionment, to a sense of the futility of the struggle, to the inevitability of a coming defeat.

When John's train arrived at the station, I was the only one there to greet him. The members of the government and Mycroft had met him upon his arrival on the ferry at Dover: That moment was ours alone. We embraced each other without a word, and to the great surprise of those passing by, my husband burst into tears in my arms. He confessed to me later that it was the first time he had cried since he was a boy. In those desperate sobs of a child, I felt his illusions dying with mine, the naive trust in a certainly better world, the chimera of a certain victory. That day marked the end of our youth.

3. From Mary's Diary

London, May 15, 1891
John can't seem to recover. Several days have passed since his arrival, and I'm starting to worry. He whispered to me in a faint voice that he doesn't feel up to returning to work. He can't sleep, I see him staring into emptiness during the day, and his face is devoid of expression, motionless, unrecognizable. He is a brave man who faced death at Maiwand and recovered from the horrifying shocks he had to endure, then and on many other occasions. He is certainly not someone who lets himself be overwhelmed by grief without reacting. Yet, this time it has happened. The courageous officer who stayed on the battlefield to save lives before being shot down, who risked death in a hospital bed, abandoned by everyone, who found the strength to recover and start again in England and eventually begin a wonderful life with me, is destroyed. I must help him, but how? Certainly not with a pat on the back and an invitation to go on living, certainly not by reminding him that at least our lives must continue. I must come up with an idea.

London, May 17, 1891
This morning at breakfast, I asked John to accompany me. He didn't object and, with a sad smile, he prepared to follow me, not knowing where or why. It was all indifferent to him. A cab dropped us off near the Victoria Dock, in front of some empty warehouses that are now used by trade unions as offices and meeting places. I pretended indifference but entered decisively. However, I observed my husband and noticed a moment of perplexity that thrilled me with pleasure: a reaction, finally.

Inside the warehouses, I turned into a corridor and found myself facing a room full of people. "Good morning," I said.

"Allow me to introduce Dr. John Watson, my husband. From today, he is going to be a volunteer in this clinic, attending to the most severe cases and the poorest among you." Then, amidst cheers and applause, I turned to John and whispered to him, "I have worked hard on this project, and you are the only one who can carry it forward. The Cardinal and the unions will provide you with the means to work, but you must believe in it. I also feel that our life will never be the same without Sherlock Holmes, but there are people who need you. And I need you too. Will you be with me, Dr. John Watson?"

I will not easily forget his answer: the faint light that I finally saw ignite in the ocean of pain in his eyes. He took his stethoscope out of his hat, brushed my hand, and said, "At least, I will try." Then he went into a side room with the first patient, closing the door behind him.

London, May 27, 1891
Several days have passed since John's debut at the clinic. A deep wrinkle still marks his forehead, his laughter from before is but a memory, yet slowly, it seems that at least a part of my beloved John is emerging from the fog. He talks to me about his work, the cases he encounters. He is amazed by the poverty and living conditions of the dockworkers and their families. He is outraged by the injustices they face. We spend a lot of time together, we have started discussing everything as we did before the tragedy of Meiringen. I find him marveling at the enormity, as he puts it, of the work I have done and continue to do. I confessed that I never thought taking care of the poor and the destitute would consume my life like this. I started almost as a joke, and now I can hardly think of anything else. But I am happy if this has brought him back to life and has united us like never

before. Such profound sadnes as we faced together can at times even create worlds of love.

London, May 28, 1891
John confided in me that he is considering returning to his practice while continuing to work as much as is necessary at the public clinic. My husband has returned: wounded, but alive. Thank God.

4. Murder at the Port

The morning work, as always, had begun at dawn, and Johnny O'Hara grumbled as usual at that bleak hour, shivering from the dampness, wrapped tightly in his work shirt and chewing tobacco while reflecting on his existence: Who the hell made him work like a dog just to get beaten down in life? He should have been a shepherd, tending to the sheep down in Ireland, like his father and his grandfather before him. But no, he had to go seek his fortune in the capital, like millions of other poor fools like him who... Yet, there was something strange about that floating bundle! What was it, a coat perhaps? Maybe it had fallen overboard from a boat, and who knows, there might be a few shillings, some... Johnny reached out his hand and immediately let out a scream. There was a corpse in those air-filled, muddy clothes.

They brought it ashore, the three of them, after calming down the distraught dockworker. He cried like a frightened child, big and bulky as he was, that mountain of an Irishman, and he kept saying that he had nothing to do with it, they had to tell the police.

"Cut it out, Johnny," one of the three shouted. "Just look who it is."

"Patrick West, that scoundrel paid by the bosses. He got what he deserved."

"Be careful what you say! Look at his back: he was stabbed and thrown into the water already dead. I'd bet a pound against a penny. It's a bad business, and I bet they'll come after us."

"What if we throw him back in the river? A scoundrel like him, whoever sold him out did a holy thing."

"Too late, an officer is coming. And you, bite your tongue from now on if you don't want to get into trouble!"

By ten o'clock, the clinic was crowded, and I had my hands full in the waiting room, trying to maintain some order so that my husband could carry out his examinations with a minimum of calm. The idea had been a resounding success, and within a few weeks, people had started crowding into the facility. Hector Ross, the union official I had discussed the idea with, had been enthusiastic from the start, and it was thanks to him that we had overcome quite a few obstacles and prejudices.

In the end, the Cardinal's offer to contribute to the expenses of the medicines distributed under John's guidance had convinced even the most reluctant, and now the clinic was an institution among the people of the port. And it was precisely at ten o'clock, with so many people inside, that we saw several police vehicles arrive at the gate in front of us, filled with officers, and everything turned into a great confusion of whistles, shouts, sharp orders, and protests. The workers gathered in groups and, with grim faces, positioned themselves in front of the union headquarters. They didn't even ask for explanations: it was all clear to them. The police sent by the management were coming to suppress their protest with some excuse, and there was no room for discussion; there was a fight to be had. Tension rose, and the two opposing lines faced each other, amid the screams of women and the threatening murmurs of the workers. Then suddenly, a man stepped forward, straight in front of the officers. On the other side, in turn, an official I knew very well stepped forward: It was Lestrade.

"What do you want, coming in force like this? Was it necessary to provoke these people this way, risking an incident?"

"We have an arrest warrant, and we intend to execute it."

"For whom, and for what crime?"

I distinguished every word in the unnatural silence that had fallen over the square, and like me, everyone in the enraged crowd: women with children in their arms, muscular dockworkers, elderly people who were no longer fit for work, a wounded and impatient community.

"We are looking for Hector Ross. The magistrate has issued an arrest warrant for the murder of Patrick West."

A roar rose, and the group of workers shuddered as they prepared to attack. But the man in front of them spread his arms to stop them.

"Not like this, comrades! That's what they want. Stay still. We will dismantle this cowardly act: Go and notify the union lawyers."

Then he calmly turned to the inspector and presented his wrists.

"I am Hector Ross. Arrest me. This is a dirty trick; I hope you realize that."

Five minutes later, Ross was taken away in a police wagon, and the police officers began to slowly withdraw, amid the whistles of some and the contemptuous silence of others. John, who had come out of the clinic, had observed the entire scene standing next to me, with a grim expression on his face.

"Do you believe it?" I asked him when we were alone.

"As much as the sun at midnight," he replied, slamming a book on the desk. "I've been collaborating with Ross in recent weeks: I can't say I know him thoroughly, but..."

"It's certainly convenient for the company to get someone like Ross in trouble. For murder, moreover, risking the gallows. And besides, does it seem possible that they found the culprit in three hours?"

"It is indeed strange. Ah, if only Holmes were here! He would certainly know what to do and..."

"But you're here, John. You're still here."

"But I'm not up to it..."

"John Watson, listen to me carefully. You were by the side of the world's greatest investigator, you

189

accompanied him and studied his methods for years. Of course, you're not him, no one is and never will be. But you can do your part, try to get an innocent man out of trouble: If you can't do it, no one else will, especially since no one is willing to try. Do you prefer to risk failing or turn your back like Pilate?"

I must have been quite a sight, with inflamed eyes, disheveled hair, and my arms on my hips, a sight certainly different from the gentle and sensitive Mary Morstan my husband had known in Baker Street. He looked at me astounded, took me in his arms, and kissed me without restraint. Two hours later, we were at Scotland Yard, where the on-duty officers stood up when they saw John: It was the first time they had seen him since Holmes's death, and I saw long faces and downcast glances among them. Lestrade was in his office and welcomed us warmly.

"First of all, doctor, allow me to express my personal sorrow, and that of all of Scotland Yard, for the loss of Mr. Holmes. We didn't always see eye to eye, but everyone here knows he was a genius, and there isn't a man in all of Scotland Yard who wouldn't have been honored to shake his hand."

"Thank you," John replied bravely. I, who knew him, realized he must have stifled a sob. "But I'm not here for that."

"I know: We are aware of the work you and your wife are doing down at the docks. Not that, between us, I don't appreciate it: The higher-ups wouldn't like what I'm about to tell you, but my heart certainly doesn't stand with the companies in this matter."

"But then why did you arrest him?"

"Because the magistrate ordered me to, and because all the evidence is against Ross. Doctor, there's not much to say. This West was connected to the management, considered a spy and a half-traitor by a lot of people at the port. Ross confronted him in front of everyone two days ago, and they almost came to blows: West had given the management the names of the most vulnerable workers, and now they risk getting fired. West left his house at midnight, saying he had an important appointment that was set up with a note that arrived at dinner time, which he took with him. And at dawn, he was dead. It seems he was stabbed in the back between one and three o'clock, and then they threw him into the water, a sign that the assault must have happened right at the port. Now, Ross didn't sleep at his house, as shown by the testimony of his landlady, and he says he can't say where he was. According to him, he was called by a woman for a serious matter outside the city, but the horse broke a leg and he had to come back on foot alone."

"And is it true?"

"Well, the poor beast was indeed killed, but Ross refuses to tell us the lady's name, for reasons of privacy. "

"However," my husband stubbornly retorted, "not having an alibi is not proof. If that's all there is, your so-called evidence is ridiculous: as you yourself said, many others could have wanted this West's hide."

"No doubt but none of them have been accused by the victim..."

Lestrade pulled out a folded sheet from his document folder. It had been folded several times and seemed to have been in water for a long time, judging by the stains and damage it had suffered, although whoever had opened and dried it had obviously been careful to treat it with care.

"I shouldn't even show it to you, but in memory of Mr. Holmes... It was in a hidden pocket of the victim's overcoat. It was in the water for several hours; it's a miracle that it's still readable. As you can see, things are clear. This gentleman was a bit ungrammatical, but he certainly had the virtue of clarity."

"To whoever finds this letter, it... my death. Here the paper is faded from water," my husband read aloud. "I accuse... another stain... the one who wants to kill me... again a stain ...ector."

"Clear, isn't it? There's no one else named Hector among the suspects; they had quarreled, he has no alibi. If there's a trial that will end with the gallows, it's this one."

"And I don't believe it. Besides, if Ross had killed him in a quarrel, he would have stabbed him in front, not in the back."

"Worse yet: an ambush. Premeditated murder."

"But come on!" John burst out. "You don't even know exactly what was written. For all you know, it could be 'everyone but Hector'!"

"In this regard," I intervened, "it might be worth seeing how long the unreadable space is. That way, you might understand how many letters or words have been erased. Don't you think so, Inspector?"

Good old Lestrade widened his eyes and swallowed twice while John gloated with satisfaction. He took out a ruler and started manipulating the message.

"There's space for three or four letters, unless there was a blank interval, but I don't see why. Hector. Or at most... why not? Ross Hector."

"First the surname?! And why on earth would that make sense?"

"I told you it was a bit ungrammatical. Oh, and before you come up with any other objections, Doctor, it's the victim's handwriting, we've already confirmed that. Besides, if someone had killed him after preparing a false message to accuse Ross, they certainly wouldn't have hidden it in a place where it could easily be ruined. They would have placed it at the victim's house in a prominent folder or something like that. No, dear Doctor: this time not even Sherlock Holmes himself could convince me that this man wasn't killed by Hector Ross. The reasons, whether political or personal, remain to be seen. But that's all."

5. The Investigation

I didn't even have to insist with John, and I didn't even need to take the initiative myself. He came out of the meeting with Lestrade so angry; I had rarely seen him in such a mood. He kept muttering to himself about "that buffoon" and saying "now I understand Holmes," until he stopped in the middle of the street, red-faced, and turned to me determinedly.

"Mary, it's unbearable!" he said. "This bumbling idiot wants to send an innocent man to prison based on at least questionable evidence, and you can bet that many people will try to take advantage of it. We can't let it go like this, by Jove. You've proven to be capable, and you have a group of helpers with you. Will you give me a hand?"

We immediately laid out our battle plan in a tearoom near Scotland Yard. From what I had been told at the union, we knew that the victim (they had called him a "scoundrel") had obtained a promotion to a clerk position in the management office, under the personal orders of the director, as a jack-of-all-trades and, as the union said, a lackey and spy. That's where we needed to stick our noses. We wasted no time, and Dr. John Watson, a well-known physician in the capital, swiftly presented himself with his gracious wife at the headquarters of the company's General Directorate.

The secretaries naturally started buzzing like frightened bees, explaining to us that a meeting with "Mr. Director" was absolutely out of the question without an appointment booked months in advance. My husband then applied a technique he had seen work often during his time with his friend Sherlock Holmes. Calmly, he handed the secretaries his business card after scribbling a few words on it.

"Please deliver this to the director: I await the response."

In a low voice, after winking at me, he explained that he had written on it, "*I am aware of several health irregularities,*

and it would be in the company's interest to address the matter
before the news reaches more interested parties. You have three
minutes to decide before I go to the union."

The office doors swung open as if a tornado had struck them, and my husband was immediately admitted to the inner sanctum, even greeted at the door by the director himself, a corpulent and sweaty man with a face resembling a weasel.

"Please come in, dear doctor. I must thank you for your concern. We care greatly about the health of our workers, and you have no doubt that your report will be given due consideration."

As John settled in, tasked with keeping the director engaged for as long as possible, I stayed outside waiting, with the intention of investigating West's papers in the hope of finding some clues that would help us identify the true culprit of the murder. We still had the problem of the two cumbersome secretaries, but we had made arrangements with Clara, who arrived a few minutes later, dressed as a man, looking elegant, accompanied by a handsome young man carrying a bulky camera with a tripod. Wearing a black cloak and felt hat, with an ivory-handled cane and a commanding gaze that I knew well and had already experienced in similar circumstances—she addressed the two secretaries with a suave voice, looking each of them in the eye, one after the other:

"Good morning, dears. My name is Emsley Carr, and I am a journalist from the 'News of the World.' This is my photographer assistant, Rupert."

"Good morning," the two of them replied in unison, while staring at one and then the other of the two 'men.'

"How can we be of assistance?" one of them asked.

"Easy: I'm writing an article for next Sunday's edition, which will have a huge circulation. It will be an exclusive piece on your colleague tragically killed by that unionist, and I would like to gather firsthand information from those who knew him well. You had daily contact with him, knew him well, a fine lad he was, and quite handsome, I hear. Which was his desk?"

"This one," said one of the two, pointing to the empty desk right in front of me.

"Would you be willing to give an interview? With both of your photos, of course!"

"Well, I'm not sure..." one of them started.

"The photo in Sunday's newspaper? With my name on it?" the other interrupted excitedly.

"Our names, you mean! You said you want to interview both of us!"

"But of course, with both your names and photos. There would also be a small financial compensation... but it's not appropriate to talk here in front of strangers, is it?" Clara said, nodding towards me, sitting on the sidelines. "Wouldn't there be a more private place to talk?"

"Of course, there's the assistant director's room! No one's there now, we won't be disturbed..."

They all moved to the other room. I knew I didn't have much time, especially because I had no idea what to look for. Fortunately, Clara had done well in allowing me to clearly identify West's desk. I opened all the drawers and went through all the folders on the desk. I was searching for any letters or messages that could help me, but there was nothing. Then I thought that perhaps the account books could tell me something. Locating them was easy. Drawing on my school experience, I attempted to analyze the financial situation of the past few months. I was lucky: There were some unclear transactions, large and vaguely specified expenditures, with the director's signature approving them. Next to them, in pencil, was a question mark. Had the traitorous spy turned against the director? Or more likely, was he monitoring the director's moves to later blackmail him? It was then that a flash crossed my mind: Of course, it couldn't have happened any other way... I tore out the pages with evidence of the discrepancies, put everything back in place, and sat back at my spot. Shortly after, Clara, the photographer, and the secretaries returned, bidding each other farewell cordially. Clara said as she left,

"Remember, 'The News of the World' next Sunday! I'll have an entire page with this scoop! Thank you and see you soon!"

"Thank you," the two girls replied in unison, watching them leave with dreamy eyes.

Soon after, John appeared at the director's door, with the director accompanying him to bid farewell.

"Thank you again, Doctor, you have been invaluable, I am very grateful to you..."

"You'll be less grateful after answering my questions!" I interrupted, standing up.

"Who are you? What do you want?"

"She is my wife," John intervened, "and I advise you to listen to her as well. She is very astute, much more than I..."

"These papers, which I'll hold here at a safe distance from you, and protected by my strong husband, could be very compromising for you, dear Director! If the experts at Scotland Yard confirm it, they are evidence of your disloyalty to the company, as well as your greed. But there's more: if, as I suspect, poor West, who had discovered everything, was blackmailing you, they are also the motive for the crime, on which you left your signature, dear Dir-*ector*! Forget H-*ector*!"

"You! How dare you stick your nose into those papers! You couldn't! Where were the secretaries? I'm calling the police now!"

"Well, you haven't understood at all," John intervened, "*we* are the police. Or almost. It's over for you. Inspector Lestrade is a good friend of ours, and if you were to call him, we would be very happy. In fact, you know what? We'll go to him as soon as we leave here, and... but where are you going?"

The director pushed John aside to make his way towards the exit and hastily fled down the stairs.

"Another clue of his guilt. He won't get far, especially in this neighborhood and especially after it's known why he ran away. Who knows if he'll make it to Scotland Yard in one piece!" John concluded with a bitter smile.

6. From Mary's Diary

London, June 10, 1891

I am about to face my most significant adventure, and I do it with indescribable anguish. I thought the worst was over and that my renewed understanding with John was the right way to help him find his balance after the tragic loss of his dear friend. But I was wrong. My new and urgent commitment will be to help John prepare for a new, unbearable pain.

I have been having doubts about my health for some time. The periods when I felt weak, suddenly devoid of energy, my easily exhausted state that forced me to stop in the middle of an activity, have become more frequent and made me fear that my constitution, like my poor mother's, is deeply undermined.

Now I have certainty: yesterday when I saw the blood on my handkerchief after a coughing fit, I understood. There was no need for the opinion of the pulmonologist, whom I rushed to see, to know what it was. I had seen too many cases of consumption over the years to have any doubts. His clinical assessment was only necessary to know how much time I still have before leaving John completely alone. And the answer was the worst possible: a few months, he told me, certainly less than a year.

And tonight we also have Lestrade for dinner, who wants to congratulate John on the successful outcome of our recent adventure. Fortunately, Rachel knows how to cook. Where will I find the strength to smile as if nothing were wrong, I don't know: at the moment, and I know it's a terrible thought, I wish it were all already over.

7. Cherchez la femme

That evening, the imminent visit of Lestrade had put John in evident agitation. Partly because it had been a long time since we had had the inspector as a guest in our home, and partly because he couldn't wait to share his enthusiasm for my investigative abilities with him. For two days, he had been showering me with compliments on how I had conducted the entire investigation by his side, praising my courage and the like-mindedness that allowed us to act as one. It was clear that he was trying to fill his insurmountable void by drawing on me.

Lestrade arrived with a bottle of white Burgundy, with which we celebrated because it seemed perfectly suited to the evening's menu: cold crouton with potted shrimps and salmon fillets with oyster sauce. The dinner concluded with a traditional Jewish dessert, which Rachel cooks wonderfully: *Haman's ears*, filled with poppy seeds. It is said that this dessert celebrates a victory over an enemy, making it very appropriate for the evening.

Lighting a cigar in the living room, where, exceptionally, I had also been "admitted," Lestrade began:

"Dear madam, your cooking is always of the highest level, and with the arrival of this girl, it has gained an international touch that makes it truly sought after. Many compliments! And congratulations to you too, Doctor, for how you conducted the investigation in which we were about to make an unforgivable mistake."

"Thank you," I replied, "I can confirm that if it weren't for Rachel, tonight you would have risked eating sandwiches. I've been feeling very tired for some time now and the girl is a precious help."

"I also thank you," John intervened, "but to be honest, this brilliant operation cannot be attributed solely to my merits. I want to emphasize that Mary did a great deal of the work, especially by way of deduction. She never ceases to amaze me."

"Well," Lestrade continued, puffing on his cigar with a sense of importance, while I opened the window so that we could still see each other in the fog, "this gives me the right to pose a problem that has me puzzled. I have a murder case and I am at a loss where to begin. Yesterday evening, the body of a woman was found in Regent's Park. She was shot in the chest at close range, presumably about an hour before the chance discovery by a citizen walking his dog. No other signs of violence or struggle. Her handbag was next to her, intact, with the purse containing money. Her jewelry, rings, and earrings were not stolen. Only a silver locket was torn away, one of those that opens, of modest value. But she might have lost it in the excitement of an altercation that left no other visible marks. No witnesses and no one who heard the shot. The killer probably knew her because she left the house in a hurry after receiving a note delivered by a messenger, telling her sister, with whom she lived, that she had an appointment.

"I immediately thought of a crime of passion, a husband with a double life who kills her to get rid of her, or because she is jealous, or even because she has discovered his infidelity. The husband is quite handsome:

tall, athletic, refined manners, a good speaker too, and very elegant. Combining his personal qualities with his social position, we could almost call him irresistible. So, I put him under pressure, investigating mainly his professional life because, given his job, he would have had the opportunity to meet numerous women: he's a lawyer, and he certainly has constant opportunities with secretaries and clients. I questioned the husband's colleagues at work, hoping to find some flaws in his impeccable image, but the more I asked, the more I found confirmation that I was dealing with a man of rare and solid moral principles, deeply in love with his wife even after ten years of marriage. Furthermore, it's worth noting that he has an alibi for that evening, as he stayed late at the office with several colleagues to prepare an important case.

The wife, too, appeared irreproachable. She had a normal social life, spending time with her husband or friends, with some other relationships, but always within the realm of a respectable bourgeois existence. No one had ever seen her with other men, and when she went out alone, she usually had her sister accompany her, whom she genuinely cared for and who was known to be equally affectionate.

I couldn't find any possible motive in their lives that could explain what happened, except for an act of absurd madness. However, if that were true, it would make it impossible for us to find the culprit. Do you have any suggestions?"

John remained silent for a moment, mentally reviewing the inspector's account. Then he spoke,

"I really don't know. It seems like there's nothing to grasp in order to identify the murderer..."

I lifted my head from the embroidery in my lap, which had kept me occupied during Lestrade's exposition.

"Yet there's a hypothesis you're struggling to find because you're referring to the 'murderer' in the masculine form. But what if I told you: *Cherchez la Femme*?"

"A woman? But who? And why? I'm absolutely certain that the husband doesn't associate with other women, completely certain!" exclaimed Lestrade.

"What was in the missing locket?" I asked.

"Nothing much. On one side, there was a photo of the husband, and on the other side, a picture of their wedding. It seems that both spouses had eyes only for each other, aside from usual social friendships," replied Lestrade.

"Very well. We know that the woman became excessively agitated upon reading the note, to the point where she took no precautions when leaving the house in the evening. It's a rather imprudent behavior, don't you think? Justifiable only in a case of absolute emergency. And in such a closely bound couple, what event could have been so catastrophic as to agitate the woman to that extent?" I continued.

"A sudden illness of the husband!" exclaimed John.

"Correct, but in that case, the woman would have gone to the hospital and would have sought the company of her sister. Instead, she went alone. The news was not meant to be shared even with the person she held dearest after her husband. It must have been devastating and scandalous news for her."

"Well, in such a case, news of an affair would fit these characteristics precisely. But we ruled it out!" said Lestrade.

"We, yes, certainly, but only after you, Inspector, investigated extensively into the husband's personality, his acquaintances, and his behavior. But how could the woman have been equally certain? How could she, if a woman pretending to be her friend, pretending to inform her out of pity or female solidarity, had written to her, 'I have evidence of your husband's infidelity, come to the park in half an hour?' That's why she neglected all precautions," I replied.

"Okay. Let's say this reconstruction gives us an explanation of how the woman was lured out of the house. But why kill her? It still remains a motiveless murder," reflected Lestrade.

"But why did you ask about the locket?" John asked.

"Excellent! You hit the mark," I exclaimed. "The locket precisely explains the motive. However, even in this case, you don't get it because you think like men. Remember what Holmes always said: He was able to meticulously reconstruct the actions of criminals at the crime scene because he could empathize with the wrongdoer, that is, he could reason like them. This murderer deeply hated a woman she might not have even known, to the extent of inventing a non-existent affair and then, perhaps because something happened that she perceived as an unforgivable offense, even killing her.

"So, trying to empathize, I imagine a woman fascinated by a man whom you yourself, Lestrade, described as irresistible. Perhaps a secretary or a client who consulted him professionally. Probably good-looking herself, very self-assured, she tried to win him over, first subtly and allusively, then with increasingly explicit behavior and conversations that inevitably struck against an impregnable wall. Self-esteem? Resentment for being rejected? Disbelief at something that had never happened to her until that moment? I don't know. What I do know for certain is that for a certain type of woman, self-assurance, personal value, even identity, we could say, depends on her power of seduction. Encountering someone who resists like this man did can provoke a completely irrational reaction, a boundless malice. Taking the locket was therefore a symbolic demonstration that the once enviable couple no longer existed."

"But why not take it out on him, then? After all, if he's the one who rejected her, right?"

"I've considered that: Indeed, she was even more malicious. By killing the woman, she struck them both at once: the woman, envied for having what was denied to her, and the man, who would be inconsolable for having lost his great love. Look for a woman in the husband's environment with the characteristics I've just described, corner her, and force her to confess. You have the experience, I'm sure you know how to do it."

"I am truly amazed. Dr. Watson was not exaggerating at all when he praised you. It feels like Holmes is again amongst us. Thank you immensely for the splendid dinner, for the delightful company, but above all, for the very enlightening lesson." With these words, Lestrade stood up and bid us farewell.

We went to bed holding each other tightly, in silence. John looked at me ecstatically and almost in disbelief. I felt that he had run out of words to express his admiration.

I later learned that the next day, by deploying all his best men, Lestrade had managed to select several ladies, some of whom had already been questioned as witnesses, and subjected them all to further interrogation. He confessed that, despite trying not to be too influenced by prejudice during the interrogations, he was immediately struck by the woman who later turned out to be the murderess. He said to me, "It was as if she had been photographed by you! I just had to treat your hypotheses as certainties."

It turned out that the woman would have been satisfied with the first part of her plan if the lady had believed her story and abandoned her presumably unfaithful husband. But the lady had not trusted her; she had demanded solid evidence, forcing the murderess to improvise. In her confusion the murderess had contradicted herself and attributed to the husband a behavior that he, a devout Jew, would never engage in: working on a Saturday, something the wife knew to be absolutely impossible. Then the lady calmed down, regained her composure, regained trust in her husband, and realized that she had been a victim of a plot, for whatever obscure reasons but certainly a plot. And she started to laugh, as if she had discovered that it had only been a nightmare. That laughter sealed her fate: At that moment, the madwoman understood that she had lost and that she would subsequently become the object of scorn and ridicule. And she did the only thing that allowed her to delude herself into thinking that she hadn't completely failed. She had torn the medallion from the victim herself, after killing her, so that she could believe that she had destroyed that perfect couple.

8. An Unexpected Miracle

Several months have passed since the case of the murderer in the park, months in which I have been able to do little else but focus on my fragile health. I agreed with the Cardinal to hand over the coordination of all my activities supporting the poor to Polly, who is familiar with the environment, is Catholic, and has matured a lot recently. John has temporarily suspended his clinic work at the docks and only visits patients at home if they are truly critical. The rest of the time, he is always with me.

Since I have daily episodes of hemoptysis and have stopped leaving the house, the gravity of my situation is clear to him as well. Initially, when I informed him of the diagnosis, he refused to accept it and immersed himself in studies to find a cure that could save me. I understand it; it's a reaction I also had when faced with an impending death. But then one calms down and resigns oneself. It's simply a matter of accompanying the patient towards the end of their suffering, trying to alleviate their pain as much as possible. And that is precisely what John is doing with me now. I let him, both because having him by my side gives me real relief and because I know it is equally vital for him as it is for me.

So, when a few days ago a note arrived from Mycroft summoning him urgently to the Ministry for "State" matters, and he got upset about Sherlock Holmes's brother lack of tact, I understood, but I also tried to calm him down.

"Can you believe it? How arrogant, as always! State affairs! There is no affair more important than those concerning your well-being, and he knows it well. He has always acted this way, even with his brother, like the elephant he is, not caring about what he tramples over..."

"Don't be like that, John. Maybe it truly is important business for which he genuinely needs your help..."

"Imagine that, that presumptuous man asking for my help. But you know, since Holmes disappeared, after the first few days when I was always in Pall Mall, he hardly received me anymore. I stopped going because it was pointless: The few times he saw me, I embarrassed him, and he couldn't wait to send me away. Maybe because I reminded him of his brother, who knows..."

"Anyway, now go, dear. Even if he was rude, you're not like that. You have always been a gentleman, and I want you to continue to be one. Although I'm so glad that you never want to leave me. But don't worry; today I'm better. The cough seems to have given me a respite. And I have Rachel here, just in case."

So John went to see Mycroft, intending to spend as little time as possible there. After a while, I heard the doorbell ring.

Rachel went to answer it, and from the bed, I sensed a commotion. I rang my bell to have Rachel explain what was happening. She came in, still arguing loudly with an elderly gentleman, rather poorly dressed, bent over and leaning on a cane.

"I told you that you cannot disturb the lady! What does it take to make you understand?"

"But the Cardinal sent me, for help, for a very difficult case that only the lady can solve..."

"Rachel, leave, thank you," I intervened with a weak voice. "Go ahead. I'll hear the gentleman out, even though there is little I can do because of my health."

Rachel left us alone. The elderly man closed the door, even though I hadn't asked him to do so, and then straightened up to his full height, removing his wig, false beard, and mustache: He was Sherlock Holmes! I didn't faint just because I was already lying down, but I still felt weak.

"Holmes, but how? Why? And why did you and Mycroft send John away with an excuse?"

"As sharp as ever, Mrs. Mary, congratulations. I'm not used to conversing with a superior intellect anymore. I will tell you what I can tell you. There are other things I must keep silent about for reasons of State, the true ones this time... At the Reichenbach Falls, I managed to escape, while Moriarty met the end he probably deserved. I couldn't reveal myself immediately, though, because I too have to follow orders.

"The real problem is not so much Moriarty's gang, although they still need to be completely dismantled, but the balance of power in Europe is at stake. It's a difficult time; we have enemies everywhere, especially me, and I am fighting them incognito. I have extremely powerful enemies in the intelligence services of many other countries. I currently live in France, but Mycroft, who has known everything from the start, informed me of your precarious state of health, and I could not refrain from coming to offer you my comfort."

"How dare you? Do you know what hell John and I have been through? And Mrs. Hudson? Do you know how much pain you could have spared us? I am very angry with you, Holmes, there is no excuse!"

"Actually, I understand it perfectly well, and I apologize. I have also suffered, like you, but I had higher orders, and above all, I had to protect both you. If you had known, you would not have been able to feign the pain so convincingly. You would have been abducted, interrogated, tortured until they discovered my whereabouts."

"But John would never have talked. He is a soldier and very courageous. And he is a man of honor."

"And would he have been just as courageous if they had tortured *you,* Mary? I don't think so. There was no other way to keep you from the same dangers I face. As for Mrs. Hudson, she will be informed soon as well. I swear I will return shortly, Mary! Just a few more months, maybe weeks, and my mission will be over, and John will know everything. Hold on, I beg you!"

"I'm afraid I have only a few hours left."

"I sincerely hope that's not the case, but if it is, I promise that I will never leave him again. Never, as long as I feel that he needs me."

"The comfort you have brought me, Holmes, is precisely this: For myself, I feel ready to go, especially because I'm suffering greatly. But I couldn't find peace regarding John's fate. Alone, completely alone, without the two of us, I had no idea how he would manage. But now you tell me that you will definitely return, and so John will have little time to despair. That is the true consolation. And for that, I thank you. I can depart with a thread of hope."

"I have come with the same hope. as well. Have a safe journey, Mrs. Mary. You will remain in my heart forever, not just in your husband's," said Sherlock Holmes.

And as he spoke, he donned his fake hair, beard, and mustache, hunched over, shrunk by thirty centimeters, and leaning on his cane, he limped away from where he had come. But I couldn't help but notice a hint of tears in his eyes.

9. From Mary's Diary

London, May 20, 1892
Dear John, this time I write directly to you in my diary because it is to you that I will leave it, along with the notes on my cases, so that you may find all my love for you within it. You will have to wait a year after my death to open it because only then will the time be ripe for me to reveal things that would endanger you if known today. Reading this, you will understand that even I

- as I imagine you - was not entirely convinced that this was truly the best choice, but I feel compelled to say that in the end, I embraced it.

From reading these pages and the others, you will come to understand many things that are currently obscure to you. Such as the strange summons from Mycroft at the Ministry to tell you things you already knew. When you returned, we calmly spoke of my imminent death, and you sensed a newfound serenity within me. Through these pages and what will unfold, you will understand why.

At that moment, I was only able to say these words to you, which I repeat now and which serve as my spiritual testament to you:

"Destiny always holds surprises. For you, they have been terrible surprises so far, but you mustn't stop hoping. Providence exists, believe me. Always believe in it, my love, and you will always find me by your side."

With love,

Yours

Mary

THE END

Stefano Guerra is a child neuropsychiatrist, psychoanalyst, professor, and retired school headmaster. He is the author of theatrical texts and film scripts, and he founded "Uno Studio in Holmes," the Italian Sherlockian Society, of which he was the president. He is a member of the Baker Street Irregulars and has authored several articles published in Italy and abroad, as well as a Sherlockian encyclopedia (with Solito).

Enrico Solito is a pediatrician and child neuropsychiatrist. He is the past president of Uno Studio in Holmes, the first Italian member of the Baker Street Irregulars, and a member of other Sherlockian associations. He has co-authored with Stefano Guerra the only Italian Sherlockian encyclopedia, as well as apocryphal Holmes stories and novels set in different contexts.

Mauro Castellini is a Los Angeles-based film producer. Born in Mantova, Italy, after obtaining his master's degree in communication sciences at Milano's IULM, he moved to Rome, where his film career took off. Having been introduced to Holmes's world by his friends Mr. Solito and Mr. Guerra, he's now teamed up with them to write this book, that marks his literary debut.

Gian Luca Guerra was born in Rome to a family connected to the film and cultural industries, in which he has passionately worked his entire life. Inspired by a story he found interesting, he joined Stefano Guerra, Enrico Solito, and Mauro Castellini in writing "The Adventures of Mary Morstan Watson."

Printed in the USA
CPSIA information can be obtained
at www.ICGtesting.com
LVHW091830161223
766618LV00032B/1463/J